VIC VALENTINE FEVER DREAMS

Will Viharo

Seattle, WA

VIC VALENTINE FEVER DREAMS

Originally published in serialized form at www.thisdesperatecity.com

Cover art by Dyer Wilk

Formatting by Rik Hall – WildSeasFormatting.com

ISBN-13: 978-0-578-92513-4

First Printing
Printed in the United States of America

Published by Thrillville Press

www.thrillville.net
www.willviharo.com

Dedicated to the Memories of

WAVERLY FITZGERALD

and

DERRICK FERGUSON

Authors and Friends

FOREWORD

By J.J. Sinisi

I should've known it wasn't a simple thing. When you ask someone, especially someone you think you know but don't *really* know, to do something you aren't quite sure how to even do yourself, how could it be simple? Some folks would call that a leap of faith.

Of course faith, God, religion, it-all-happens-for-a-reason triteness, none of those old platitudes exist in Will Viharo's world, or more appropriately, in the kaleidoscope existence he creates and also somehow inhabits at the same time.

To read a Vic Valentine adventure, to strap on a pair of crisp Oxfords and a faded plaid suit, to move within the ethereal wisps of his bastards, babes, and brutes, is to steep yourself not just in the wonderful imagination of his creator and author, Will the Thrill, lounge lizard, tiki foreman, and b-movie socialite, but it's also the act of prying down the slats of moonlit venetian blinds and spying into the complex psyche of the actual man named Will Viharo.

What the hell does that even mean? Will the Thrill, Will Viharo, and Vic Valentine are all different aspects of the same person. Actually, no, that's not true at all. The three of them are independent explorations of retroist theory from totally different perspectives: he who fetishizes it, he who heals from it, and he who lives it.

It's a mindfuck really.

But shit if that's not what makes it so damned interesting. And not simple. Not simple at all.

A quick story.

Let's cut out the traumatic early years, the parents, the years on the beat, the trying-to-make-it-in-this-town overtones. Words flitter by, written, rewritten, published. Characters are born, they fuck, they get shot and they die die die.

Then about a decade ago, Christian Slater walks through a beat-up bookshop and flips through a creased paperback novel and on the spot decides it's so good he wants to explore its film options.

That's not a real story, is it? It is when it doesn't get optioned, even after Cuban cigars, action figures, boat trips, and a cruel bait and switch.

You catch if that happened to Will, Vic, or the Thrill? Me neither.

Here's another one. Some dude skins a bat and then eats it. He gets sick. Coughs on the chick next to him. She gets sick. Fast forward. Chinese New Year. International flights. The NBA cancels a season. The world shuts down. Like the whole fucking world. And an average dude who's been published in the trades and also runs a crime fiction website suddenly has a couple extra minutes, because, you know, pandemic. He picks up a novel from an author he once shared a title page with and reaches out.

Will, he asks, you up for creating something experimental, short, with pictures, and maybe some social stuff?

Will says he'll think about it. Maybe he's not ready to cut open the veins and bleed those tales of woe so soon after the last time. Maybe it's not that simple for him either.

But then he balks, because all good PI's can't resist an opportunity. Vic Valentine is resurrected once again, twisting his way through reality in a weekly serialized Instagram experiment.

That one has to be the Thrill, doesn't it?

Wrong.

The story drips onto Instagram, a weird laboratory platform for storytellers but worth a go. *Fever Dreams* it's called. It comes out every week. Every. Fucking. Week. For over a year, the author who lives retro, breaths class, and takes every gritty punch life gives him square in the nose, delivers a thrilling, introspective, impassioned, time travel journey that manifests the shared fears of isolation, sadness, freight, and hope brought on by this very shitty reality we can't escape.

And that's the best thing about *Fever Dreams*, and why when I approached Will to write whatever he wanted, however often he wanted, and without any restraints, I never would have dreamed he'd deliver something so moving, so complex. So not simple.

The trick here is we decided to keep each episode short. Real short. Three hundred words short. That brings out the Hemingway.

Fever Dreams isn't escapism. It isn't a wild adventure to distract its loyal readers from the pain and death all around them. But it isn't indulgent of these fears either, despite occasionally taking place in and around the environs of their reality, the ventilators, the zoom meetings, their shackled planet.

Vic Valentine is trying to solve a mystery while romping through time and twisting imagery, seeing the devil, dead lovers, and scorching hot fevers. Will the Thrill laments a lost year's worth of opportunities to honor those whom his lounge lizard act is a pastiche of a bygone era. Will Viharo is right beside us, me really, trying to make sense of a picture that's so upside down we don't even remember what shape it was in the first place.

Because that's the answer to all of it. That's the brilliance and the entertainment of *Fever Dreams*, and actually, all of this man's works. The twisted brambles of his multiple identities drives a very specific, and very personal, imaginative exploration.

I asked Will Viharo, the author, if he could deliver short, concise tales, and if possible, make them about his buddy Vic. I didn't know what I was in for, but I should've. I should've known a person charging through the burning fire of life would always deliver something exemplary.

I should've known it wasn't a simple thing.

Joe Sinisi
Caged on Long Island
May 2021

Joe Sinisi is a published short story writer, mostly

crime fiction and mostly at the places you know. Now he spends his time reigniting his noir website *This Desperate City* while partnering with authors to push and promote their work. He's currently working on a sprawling medieval saga that has very little to do with crime, but everything to do with very bad people.

THE LAST TIME

You never know these days when you do anything if it's for the last time. So I just keep jerking off in defiance of death. It's the perfect quarantine pastime. It's not an antidote to loneliness, though. Never was. Trust me. I'm an expert in both.

Since the crisis started my dog walking gigs have dried up like pooch piss on a sunny sidewalk, and of course my private eye days are long behind me, unless you count my existential examination of Life. That's an ongoing mystery. Few clues to share right now, sorry. The world is always one step ahead of me, making it hard to follow. I was always lousy at surveillance, anyway.

Now everyone is getting laid off. I'm still trying to get laid, or get off. That was always hard to do, even before social distancing, one trend I actually pioneered, but as usual, nobody knows it but me.

I got my share of poon tang, I guess. But as I grow older, I find myself masturbating to memories of sex more than actually creating new ones. Life is not a gourmet buffet. Like presidential elections, it's often a case of choosing between bad and worse. Like growing old vs. dying young. Not sure, but I think I'm in the high risk demographic for this thing. My underlying condition is I'm a loser by nature. That tends to undermine one's chances of beating anything, except one's self.

On the bright side of this *noir* equation, I'm a pretty pessimistic person anyway. I doubt I'd ever test positive for anything, except negativity.

I'm lost in this morbid contemplation of my own doom mixed with mental images of Bettie Page when the phone rings again. My smartphone. Yes, I have one, though I'm not as smart as it is. Not entirely sure how it works, but I can take pictures with it and talk on it, too. Look at me, figuring things out for myself.

I answer it because what the hell, a voice is a voice, and that's always good these days, especially if it's coming from outside your own head. Not sure who it could be. I hardly know anyone in Seattle even though I've been here for years. Hard to maintain associates in this gloomy town, even if I wanted to. Relationships hit icebergs even in the warmest conditions. It's called the Seattle freeze. Ironically, that's one reason I moved here from San Francisco so long ago. Some like it cool. I've always avoided eye contact, except for actual eye contacts, unless there was a hot body attached. Now all anyone lusts after is antibodies.

I suppose that's crude and sexist. But in a global pandemic, it's petty to pick on our human faults and foibles. We're all going to die, anyway. If not this, something. So what if we're bastards. Nature doesn't care. It's not personal. Okay, maybe it is.

I'm half hoping my missing wife in on the line. But no, just music again. So maybe it is. Once more, like old times, it's the sound of a scratchy 45, not the kind you shoot yourself with after swilling a bottle of tears. Sinatra singing "The Last Dance." I put it to my ear and get up and dance around the dingy little room by myself, Billy Idol style, the cheap dive's red neon sign beaming from outside the window like a satanic spotlight. Once the song ends, as it always does, the caller, no ID, hangs up. I try dialing *69 but that doesn't work on these fancy 21st century pocket computers.

Years ago, in the previous century, pre-pandemic—the cultural divide in our common consciousness— a stalker I labeled The Phone Phantom used to leave me these mysterious musical messages on something called an answering machine. I had no idea who it was, though I had my suspicions, until I met Val, my missing wife, who confessed. She was courting me from the shadows of my consciousness long before we met 'n' married. I hope she still is on my trail, wherever she's hiding now.

I remember the last time we kissed, the last time we made love, the last time we watched movies together. The last time we laughed. I wish I had her here with me now, I mean in physical form, not this spiritual jazz. Solitude for me was a thing of the past, I thought. Now it's everyone's present. A present we'd all like to re-gift.

So I jerk off again, thinking of Val and Bettie Page and all my many lovers, real or imagined, trying to get a grip on reality, but it keeps slipping through my sticky fingers, despite my ennui-induced erections.

I can't remember the last time anything was this hard.

NEXT!

We're rolled onto the treadmill as soon as we're spit out of the oven. Death is already waiting to pop us into its mouth one by one, like Lucy and Ethel in that chocolate factory bit. Something is going to eat us alive, sooner or later. Just a matter of when we get snatched off the assembly line. Then we're chewed up and swallowed back into the belly of the beast, shat and flushed down the cosmic drain into the eternal sewer.

I don't know about you, but I'm afraid of Death. Life scares me too, but Life is a foe I know. It's the unknown killer lurking in the shadows that keeps me perpetually paranoid. Sometimes that paranoia flares into panic, which isn't helped by all the chaos and suffering on TV. I turn off the news to watch *giallo* movies instead. Stylized sex and murder, Italian style, is so soothing by comparison. Sometimes I just stare into space, waiting to disappear.

Like now, gazing with passive sadness at the eerily tranquil still life of Puget Sound outside my window, which is as deceptively quiet and peaceful as a beautiful butchered corpse floating face down in the water, an oblivious heron hitching a ride on her ice cold back as they both float in the misty sunlight.

I don't have a thermometer other than my dick, but I know I have a fever and chills. Not the kind I get watching Edwige Fenech stretched out nude. More the kind that means I just got slashed down the middle by an unseen stalker. I don't have a cough. But my throat is sore as hell, I got pink eye, and I'm shitting more than Satan after a day's worth of devouring sweet little souls.

I think back on my life as I sit there in the dark, a blanket around my shivering shoulders, jazz on the radio, a near empty bottle of bourbon on the nightstand. I'm too tired to even dream of better times.

Doesn't stop me from hallucinating them, though.

TEMPERATURE CHECK

I'm thrusting my thermometer into her furiously when I wake up and realize I've been humping my pillow, which is now soaking wet, and not just from sweat. My dream girl has evaporated in the gray light of day again.

I've been there too many times. I've been here, too. Now I don't know the difference between here and there.

Everybody knows the truth, and the truth is, nobody knows.

My cellphone pings, meaning I got a text message, so it ain't music again.

It says, "Test results positive."

The sender is Unknown. I suspect the nature of the test being referenced. I just don't remember being tested. I've already been self-diagnosed as a chronic hypochondriac. It's a fatal condition that is simply taking its time, because eventually, my fear of dying, especially alone, will confront my actual agent of Death.

My little dark room is full of monsters. Most of the time they're invisible, but after I shiver and sweat enough, trying to sleep, I can see them, eyes wide open.

I grew up watching horror movies. Now that I'm living a dystopian nightmare, they're mere manifestations of the ghouls haunting my psyche all along. They don't scare me. I just want them to leave me alone.

I'm gonna be killed by a monster, I'd rather it be one of those bosomy lesbian vampires from an old Hammer flick. Of course, since she's a lesbian, she won't enjoy the sex as much as I will, but she'll enjoy my demise much more, so it'll even out. I don't believe in taking advantage of women. The pleasure must be mutual.

I feel my forehead. It's on fire. I swig the rest of the bourbon then rub the bottle all over my face, pretending it's the fleshy breast of an undead succubus, cold and firm. But empty, devoid of soul.

I suck it dry, beating it to the punch. But it's the only medicine I have. Now it's gone. Time to venture out for a refill. Wish me luck.

THE WORLD BEFORE

Wait. I can't leave my room. I'm sick, contagious. Plus I hate people. Been trying to avoid them all my life. Now they do it for me. Makes it easier.

I've even social distancing in my dreams. Except for the wet ones.

There's nobody out there on the streets. It's dark now. Maybe it's safe to sneak into a market and grab some groceries and booze.

I can't remember how I even wound up in this hotel, alone. Last thing I recall is being home with my wife. There was no pandemic. The only plague on Earth was humanity. Now Nature was reasserting dominance. The air is cleaner, animals are happier. Only people are suffering. I have empathy only because I'm one of them.

I could just sit here and stare at myself fading away in the dirty mirror. Or just watch TV. They only have three channels. News, horror movies, and porn. The essentials.

At least I have some cash. Fuck it. I go down to the front desk. The dude is wearing a mask. Not the surgical kind. He looks likes a mutation, a hideous freak. I just keep walking, outside into the silent night.

I see a neon sign that says OPEN. It's actually a bar. The news said they were all closed. I'm curious. I go to the door and see another sign: INFECTED ONLY.

A big bouncer comes out and stops me once I pull on the handle. He's a monster. Literally. He looks me over carefully, sizing up my signs of physical illness. I see a stripper dancing on a stage behind him. Her body is perfect. Her face is a nightmare.

I'm reminded of Times Square in the late 70s and early 80s, when I was a young hotshot journalist, before I became a private eye. It was a neon-lit hellhole, full of smut and vermin and viruses and bodily fluids, everyone crammed together, sweating, bleeding, cumming.

Dying.

Feels like home again as I walk inside.

DEAD DREAMS

If you live your life in constant fear of dying, you might as well already be dead. I was dead inside anyway. The rest would catch up soon enough, one way or another. Maybe I shouldn't be patronizing this place, even though it's a sanctuary for Infected only. I'm not even positive I'm positive for the virus. But the bouncer seemed to think so, and I need the company, and the booze. It's my only medicine.

What the hell. Life has always been a series of calculated risks.

I'm just sitting on a stool staring at my drink, wondering why I'm even here. I don't mean the bar. The planet. The shapely but grotesque stripper on stage keeps gyrating to songs by The Cramps. The bar is dark and ancient, lined with leather booths and velvet paintings of naked Tahitian girls. There's a tiki statue inside a glowing fountain in one corner. It's leering at me, like Death. I give it a nod. It just keeps grinning.

There's hardly anyone else around. The few here are in booths, hidden in shadows. I'm almost alone at the bar. One guy sits at the other end, his deformed face mostly hidden from me as he contemplates his own drink without sipping, as if wondering whether to dive into a pool of acid or just hope things get better.

Like me, he's probably thinking of everything that might've been, pre-pandemic. But it wasn't the virus that killed off our dreams. It was Life itself.

I sip my tropical bourbon cocktail, recalling my mother dying in an insane asylum, my dirty cop father getting shot down in an alley, my older brother jumping off the Brooklyn Bridge. My many long lost loves. My self-aborted career as a journalist, my long, fruitless so-called career as a private eye. My days as a dog walker.

All gone now.

Then the guy at the end of the bar looks up at me and says, "I need someone to find the cure. You want a job?"

LAST CALL

The guy with the fucked-up face sidles over next to me. He's wearing an overcoat and he smells bad. I social distance another seat down, but he doesn't follow me. He gets it.

He motions to the bartender to refill both our tiki mugs. The bartender also has a corpse-like countenance. He doesn't talk much. When I ordered my cocktail I just pointed to the menu and he nodded. I miss my old pal Doc Schlock, proprietor of The Drive-Inn down in San Francisco, above which was my studio apartment/office, long ago and far away, like the song. Doc was my best friend, next to my missing wife. Doc is dead, though I still see him sometimes. My wife may still be alive, but I never see her. Not lately.

"What's the name of this joint, anyway?" I ask the zombie bartender.

"Last Call."

"No, I meant, what's this place called."

He just stares at me like I took a crap on the floor.

Fuck-face laughs. "I hear you're a dick."

"Used to be. How did you know?"

"Grapevine."

"Only sour grapes left here, pal."

"You still for hire?"

"Retired."

"This is a global emergency, if you haven't noticed."

"I'm not a scientist. Can't save the world. Sorry."

"Don't need to be an epidemiologist. Just smart."

"Then you're shit out of luck. I'm as dumb as they come."

I look over at the stripper, who is inside the fountain, humping the tiki as an old-style saxophone riffs out of nowhere.

Fuck-face doesn't seem to notice her. He taps my shoulder and says, "Listen. This job pays well. You can move out of that dump."

"I don't even know how I got there."

"You mean you have amnesia?"

"Only recently. I woke up into this nightmare. Life is just a dream, anyway. I just fell asleep on the remote."

"This is real life. And it's getting more real by the minute. Wake up and smell the death."

"Smell it often. I never inhale."

He punches me in the kisser, and I go down.

VOODOO VIRUS

The crazy, ugly guy who knocked me off my stool and wants to hire me to solve the Case of the End of the World is named Doctor Floyd Something. Or Doctor Something Floyd. There are three parts but I only caught two when he introduced himself after hitting me. I'm already drunk. I decide to order a sandwich with my next drink, but because I'm vegan, all I can eat is bread with pickles and tomatoes. Side of chips, so that's almost a meal. Still, the bourbon went to my head, but that was the intended destination anyway.

"Sorry for that," he says sincerely. "I'm on edge. And desperate. I don't understand your attitude."

"I don't need you to understand. Just don't wanna be a detective anymore. No future in it."

"No future in anything, for any us."

"There you go. Why bother. I can't even enjoy my own misery in peace these days. Too much company."

"What else you need to do with whatever time you have left?"

"Remember."

"What?"

"Everything."

"Why?"

"I want to remember my life while I'm still alive to remember it."

"Is it worth remembering?"

"It's a long joke on me with no punchline. But it's the only story I got."

"You still have time to change the ending."

"Hey pal, I don't know you who've been talking to, or how you know my personal and professional business. I also don't care. Nothing surprises me anymore and I stopped wasting questions due to an answer shortage. Despite what you might've heard, I possess no secret exorcism spell against viral virility, my volatile new friend."

"Your wife sent me."

The stripper had worked her way across the room and instead of undulating against the tiki in the fountain, she's rubbing up against me in time with a Les Baxter tune. Little Elvis sits up straight in my pants, leaking through my rumpled sharkskin suit. I loosen my skinny tie and kiss her, despite her freakish facial features.

"I ain't got a wife anymore," I tell Dr. Floyd.

ESSENTIAL SERVICES

I had a dream once I was feeling my wife's forehead for fever. I woke up, she was asleep next to me, and I felt it again. She was fine. I went back to sleep. When I woke up, she was gone, and I was alone in that hotel in the middle of a global pandemic. How long had I been out? It was the Twenties already. Again.

"She didn't run out on you," Dr. Floyd says, reading my mind, which is an open book anyway.

"She's done if before," I say with a shrug. "Disappear without notice."

"There's a plan. She still loves you."

"Good to know," I say, sipping the cocktail he bought me after socking me in the face. It took me off guard, but it wasn't very hard. I've been hit hard. This was like getting swatted with a sock full of gumdrops. It stung, but it was the shock that made me fall, not the force. The guy is old and weak, plus crazy and ugly. But I never turn down a free drink, especially during an apocalypse.

"You know she's paying your tab at the hotel," the mind-reader says. None of this may actually be happening anyway, so it makes sense he can see my thoughts. I might as well be dreaming. Maybe that's why I barely felt his punch, though I can feel the punch

I'm drinking well enough.

"Yeah, she does that sometimes too," I say. "But a lot has happened since I saw her last, when there were only rumors of a fatal flu going around. I hope she's healthy. She can live without me. I can't live without her."

"We need your skills of detection if any of us are to live."

"Why? You're a doctor, right? Nobody needs a shriveled-up dick."

"I tried. I failed. This is not a case for conventional corrective science."

"Your face sure is. The bartender and stripper, too."

He cackles. "Have you seen your own reflection lately?"

My blood runs colder than the ice in my glass as I look into the mirror behind the bar.

THE BEACH IS BLACK

I look into the mirror behind the bar, expecting to see my face transformed into that of a mutant monster, like everyone around me in this desolate little urban oasis of infected freaks. Instead I see nothing but my visage isolated in a seeming abyss. I look around and realize I am no longer inside The Last Call, or inside anywhere. I'm outside nowhere, standing alone and naked on a windswept beach at night. I am being buffeted by the strong sea breeze, pelted by large raindrops, staring out into the stormy void, barely able to see the line between the horizon and the ocean, since both are pitch black.

I begin to shiver, not so much from cold, but from fear. This must be Death. That crazy witch doctor spiked my tropical cocktail or something. Or maybe the voodoo virus finally finished me off. In any case, I am still sentient, but not quite existing, at least not in the conventional sense.

Several times during alcoholic blackouts, and later my so-called fugue states, I experienced something similar, where it seemed I was adrift somewhere in the outer limits of a twilight zone, but those trips gave me a sense of emancipation. Now I feel only dread.

Worst of all, wherever I am, I am all alone. I'd give

anything to be back inside that tiki bar of the damned. At least I'd have company. I wouldn't mind if my features had been disfigured by the disease like the rest of my fellow viral victims.

I just don't want to die alone.

I want my wife.

I want my life.

There's only one way to end this.

With stoic resignation I begin marching into the waves. They crash over me and I'm pulled under into the depths. I feel the water filling my lungs like pneumonia. It's a horrible way to go, but if I am indeed infected, this is my fate anyway.

Maybe down below, or somewhere beyond, my wife awaits, like a merciful mermaid.

SLEEPWALKING IN SEATTLE

For a long time it feels like I'm either falling through space or drifting inside a storm cloud. Lighting flashes around me, as thunder echoes in my skull. But I'm not afraid. The feeling of emancipation from all temporal concerns becomes intoxicating. Except for the loneliness. That's what pulls me back down to relative reality. I miss my wife, because I love her. I miss my life, because it feels unfinished.

Next thing I know, I'm back in my sharkskin suit and skinny tie, wrinkled but not wet, wandering the empty night streets of Seattle. The Space Needle gleams in the dark distance like a beacon to nowhere. I think I'm in the Belltown district, not far from The Last Call, the bar designated for "the infected." I can't find it. The city appears deserted, as if I'm the Last Man on Earth. I can only hope I find the Last Woman on Earth, and that she's my missing wife. We won't procreate, though. The human experiment has ended in failure. We'll just fuck and drink and wait our turn to disappear from an indifferent galaxy, leaving the Earth and its less neurotic sentient denizens in peace.

Every now and then I think I see a zombie, but I leave them alone. I touch my own face, feeling my features, fearful of deformity due to the disease. But I don't even feel sick anymore. The seawater has washed away my symptoms, or so it seems.

I try to make it back to my hotel, but that seems to have vanished too. I just keep walking, searching for a sign of Life other than my own.

In an alley I see a shapely shadow. It's feminine in form. I decide to follow her. Even if she's not my wife, maybe she can provide me with a clue, an answer, a direction, or just some companionship. I'll take what I can get.

The shapely shadow leads me down the alley into what seems to be a maze of alleyways.

Then she suddenly stops, turns and faces me, completely nude.

I recognize her.

DREAM SHADOW

The naked shapely female stranger takes my hand and leads me through more dark, interconnecting alleyways. It's like a maze inside my mind. Finally she walks us through a wooden doorway in a brick wall, like one of those secret speakeasy joints popular in L.A. years ago. We are not back in The Last Call, Seattle's hidden tiki bar of the damned. Instead, we are inside my old office/apartment above The Drive-Inn, San Francisco's combo bar/video store, now long gone.

She's not my wife. Not exactly. Rather, she appears to be an amalgamation of many women from my past, like Rose and Dolly, along with vintage screen sirens that regularly swim through my wet dreams.

Apparently, she is not real. Which makes me wonder if I am, especially now that I'm right where I was, a quarter century ago.

"Is this some Frank Capra Christmas Carol crap?" I ask her.

She shakes her head in the negative with disturbing solemnity. She doesn't talk, which means she definitely isn't one of my ex-girlfriends, or my missing wife.

Everything looks the same. The framed Mara Corday

photo on my desk. The Film Noir poster from the Roxie. The stack of Bettie Page videotapes on top of the TV. The lonely bed.

I look outside the window. It's the foggy Richmond District of San Francisco circa the 1990s, all right. There's even people. Nobody is masked, social distancing or any of that jazz.

If I've really been transported back in time, does that mean my old pal Doc Schlock (Curtis Jackson) is downstairs right now, alive and well? As a black man from Oakland, he'll be unhappy to hear about all the social unrest following his untimely death. Not surprised, though.

I look at my Dream Girl without saying anything. She nods and points toward the door. I walk past her and then run down the stairs.

The Drive-Inn is open for business, and there's Doc behind the bar, serving drinks. On the TV he's playing a movie as usual:

Out of the Past (1947).

THE FUTURE THAT NEVER WAS

Walking slowly into The Drive-Inn as if sinking into a barrel of bourbon, I take my customary seat at the bar and nod at Doc, who nods back, as if none of this is strange, at least to him. I also wink at my old gal-pal Monica Ivy, doing a tame striptease in one corner of the bar, one of Doc's attempts to boost business after video rentals started slipping, which confirms my current location as San Francisco circa the mid-1990s.

It all looks like a mirror world of The Last Call, back in Seattle circa the early 2020s. Except no one is deformed or sick. It's all beautifully normal, just as I frequently remember it. And I fully sense everything around me, as if it's truly tangible, not just a mirage of a halcyon past. My phantom escort in nowhere in sight.

Then I can't help myself. I get up just as Doc puts a beer and shot in front of me, go around the bar, and hug him. He hugs me back. He feels like flesh and bone, unlike the ethereal visage I've grown accustomed to since his death in the 2000s, about a decade hence. A few tears escape.

"Vic, you okay? Tell me, my man."

So after sitting back down I tell him everything, including about my wife, which he's happy to hear, even if he doesn't believe me. I also tell him about Dr.

Floyd and his attempts to recruit me to save the world from the pandemic, as if I were humanity's only hope.

"Freud?" Doc says.

"*Floyd.* You know, like Brad Pitt's character in 'True Romance.'"

"Vic, if some mutant quack thinks you're mankind's salvation, bouncing back and forth in time like the goddamn Terminator, obviously there's something wrong with him, way beyond the shit you're telling me."

"But it was all real, Doc. It is real. Or it will be. That's the scary thing. This, all this here and now, is just…a dream of a memory."

Doc shakes his head. "No, Vic. What you just told me, *that's* the dream. *This* is reality. Welcome back."

MEMORY OF A REVERY

I try to wrap my head around the bombshell Doc just laid on me.

"So you're saying this right now is not a dream of a memory, but what I told you is a memory of a dream?"

"That's it, my man. I mean, if you ain't real, neither am I. And I'm definitely real, motherfucker."

I feel both relieved and traumatized, because if this is true, I fell asleep and dreamed about ten years of my life that never happened. At least. In fact, more like twenty-five years, if everything after this very moment was part of that extended dream, too.

"So no pandemic? No Black Lives Matter movement? No wife?"

"All in your head, man. Black Lives Matter? Since when? Not on my watch. I god damn *wish*. More like Black Lives *Splatter*. And Donald Fucking Trump becomes our damn President? Bitch, *please*."

I'm still depressed and disoriented, but then that's always been my usual state, so in a way, Doc's radical explanation is already beginning to make sense.

"That was one long, lucid dream then," I say, mostly to myself. I gaze at Monica, still dancing for a crowd of three perverts. She waves at me, and I get a boner. Yeah, this all seems pretty real, all right. But then so did the other, future third of my life. And my missing wife, who apparently was a figment of my imagination all along. Although her backstory begins here and now, so I could always look for her in present day San Francisco...

A white-haired older man in an overcoat and floppy hat sits a couple stools down from me. He removes his hat and locks his cold blues eyes with mine, sending a chill of recognition through my skull.

"Hey Doc, you got a customer," I tell my friend behind the bar, who is busy wiping down the further end.

"Doc?" says the stranger in an eerily familiar voice. "That's funny."

"Why's that?"

"I'm a doctor, too. I don't provide his kind of medicine, though, which is what I need at the moment."

"What's your specialty?"

"Disease. I'm an epidemiologist. Floyd's the name. Harold Floyd."

BEYOND THE BLACK HOLE

Like I said, the guy is older, but he's not that old. Maybe in his 50s. But then so am I. Wait. No. It's the mid-90s so I'm only in my 30s. I do a face check in the mirror behind Doc Schlock's bar. I'm young again. My middle age was only a nightmare that still awaits.

But this can't be the same Dr. Floyd from my fabricated future, could it? Maybe it was all just a premonition.

I need to find my wife. I mean now, before I ever met and married her sometime after the turn of the century. She must have all the answers. She always does.

Meantime, I am sitting here in a time and place I thought was long gone, except in my murky memories and dead dreams. I decide to relish it, even if I am uneasy in my conviction it actually exists outside my increasingly haphazard consciousness.

This guy sitting next to me offers a clue to which reality is real, too. I decide to just ask him.

"Are you the same guy that sat next to me in that tiki bar for the infected up in Seattle around the year 2020?"

The guy who calls himself Harold Floyd looks at me with a puzzled expression, as if he is suddenly confronted with a crazy person in an intimate space. Or just another drunk. He decides to be nice about it, in any case.

"My friend, I'll be past eighty by then, and probably dead."

"Not quite. You'll just look it. We all will, because of the pandemic."

"Pandemic? You must've read my book. I am flattered."

"Your book?"

"Yes, just published. I predict the end of the world due to a pandemic combined with economic collapse, racial strife, and poor leadership."

"Not much of a dice roll. I kinda figured it would be something like that."

"So you share my vision, young man?"

Young man. Been a while since anyone called me that. "You got me, Doc. I mean, the other Doc from the other dimension."

"I actually believe you."

Fuck.

INTANGIBLE EVIDENCE

My mother died in a mental institution. I always thought I would too. Maybe that's where I am now, hallucinating all this madness. Only one way to prove I'm not lost in some delirious daydream or neurotic nightmare.

I suddenly deck Harold Floyd right off his stool, to prove to myself he's corporeal. My fist feels it, and so does his face.

Doc comes around the bar and helps him back up, apologizing, offering a free drink as compensation.

"Vic, you gotta go, man," Doc says, shaking his head. "You can't be beating up my customers. They're getting harder to come by."

"Wait till all the bars close," I say.

Floyd looks at me, rubbing his jaw, and says with a wink, "I'll pay you back for that some day." Oddly, he doesn't seem that upset. And he's alluding to something that already happened twenty-five years from now, up in Seattle at The Last Call, the only bar still open, where we will meet again.

"Yeah, I know. In about a quarter century."

He points his finger at me as a perplexed Doc nods for

me to beat it.

"See you later," Floyd says, sending a chill through my soul.

I go back up to my office to calm down and think, lying on my dirty bed like old times, or maybe still new times. I can't tell anymore. It's all a dream within a nightmare or vice versa. I'm afraid to go to sleep, since I may wake up back in the future. I want to stay here forever. But Time never stands still, in any dimension. Maybe my dream was a vision of an inevitable fate. Or I've been given a reprieve by some benevolent entity.

Bullshit.

I decide to jerk off when my old pal the Naked Dream Tour Guide from Hell suddenly reappears. She climbs into the bed and finishes the job for me. I don't even care if she's real, or I am.

She lies in my arms and kisses me until I either drift back to dreamland or return to reality.

MAZE OF MALAISE

I make love again with my Mystery Date, because what the hell, I have nothing better to do. Nothing makes sense anymore, and if it ever did, someone was lying. Probably me to myself. My sexy angel might just be another delusion, but like all the others around here, she is sensorily correct. I can feel, touch, taste and smell every inch of her. She doesn't speak, even when prompted, but she communicates with her mesmerizing eyes. Our spirits are linked. Maybe that's all we are. Lost souls. And this replica of my old apartment in 1990s San Francisco is nothing more than a movie set, a projection of the past on a celestial screen. I'm both spectator and participant.

Back in the real world, the one you think is everlasting and invincible, I remember watching a snail crawling across the sidewalk with acute fascination. All it wanted to do was survive long enough to make it to the other side. And then what? What's the point? Why struggle so hard to stay alive in a world like this?

Simple. Because it's all we sentient beings know.

Now I'm in this alternate world, and unlike the other one, I'm not alone, even if I actually am. It's the feeling that counts, even in an illusion. Especially in an illusion. Because it's all just one interconnected mass hallucination.

This is my current conclusion as we climax together again and she passes out panting and perspiring beside me. The scent of our seemingly corporeal fluids permeates my quasi-consciousness.

But as usual, even in this dimension of dementia, nothing lasts long. All moments fade into the next, and as usual the transition is fucking annoying.

The phone on my office desk rings. I let it. Then my answering machine picks up. I forgot I had one, because it's been so long since I was this young age in this idyllic era and location.

It's The Phone Phantom again, leaving a musical message. But this time, with 2020 hindsight, I now exactly who it is, and where to find her.

ANTISOCIAL DISTANCING

The strange thing about this situation—or rather, the strangest thing at this particular juncture in a series of strange situations—is that I can remember where was wife was, or rather is, in 1990s San Francisco. I only found this out after we finally hooked up for real many years later, South of the Border on a particularly strange case (strangeness has never been a stranger to me). That's when she belatedly revealed herself as The Phone Phantom, having clandestinely stalked me from afar for many years following our very first encounter, when I found a flyer about her missing cat, shortly after I'd decided rather arbitrarily to become a "private eye," and I hired myself to find it.

Naturally when I returned her pussy I hit on her. She blew me off by saying she'd never date me until and unless Donald Trump became the President of the United States. At the time that prospect was so far-fetched I interpreted her conditional response as a resounding "fuck off forever." I guess she knew something I didn't. Most people do, apparently.

Her name was Esmeralda Ava Margarita Valentina Valdez, and still is, or eventually will be, but with "Valentine" tacked on the end. I always called her Val. Ironically, when I met my first true love, Rose, her name was Valerie, and I called her Val. It all means something. Exactly what, I have no idea. I'm not that good a detective.

Anyway, since I am inexplicably back in the 1990s with futuristic memories dating up to the 2020s, I know exactly where The Phone Phantom lives, provided it's the same address as before.

The song she leaves on the machine is less cryptic than usual, now that I know her M.O. Of course, if my references are the remnants of a subconscious sojourn, my conclusions are crap.

I throw on my sharkskin suit and go to kiss my Spiritual Guide goodbye, but she's already vanished again like an erotic mirage. So I head out, Roy Orbison's "In Dreams" reverberating in my head.

THE EXTENUATING ANGLE

Wait. Where am I going?

Down the stairs from my office above The Drive-Inn, onto the street. To Val's old apartment. But I can't remember where it was, and is.

Am I already forgetting the future?

No. Our initial meeting happened before whenever Now is. I keep going, hoping it comes back to me.

Once outside, it's no longer 1990s San Francisco, but Times Square, way in the past. The cars and fashions are familiar from my distant youth.

"In Dreams" has stopped playing inside my head, replaced by "Only the Lonely" blasting from the open door of a record store I once frequented with my dead brother, before he jumped off the Brooklyn Bridge. But it isn't the Roy Orbison song. It's the totally different song with the same title, by The Motels.

I keep walking in a daze past punkers, pimps, whores, junkies and bums. Following primal instincts I turn a corner and I'm on 42nd Street, greeted by that dazzling row of neon marquees.

One says *The New York Ripper* and *Satan's Baby Doll*. Both are Italian. The first is a Fulci classic, a particularly violent and nihilistic *giallo*. The latter is a remake of *Malabimba – The Malicious Whore* (1979), blasphemous supernatural sexploitation, right up my alley.

All of this means I'm back in 1982, and only in my early twenties.

A voluptuous woman is suddenly standing in front of me wearing knee-high boots, a shiny black leather coat unbuttoned to her cleavage, and shades, which she removes to reveal herself as my Spiritual Tour Guide.

She's not Val, but I'm happy to see her. At least I'm not alone.

Wait. Who is Val again?

She has two tickets for us. She leads me inside the malodorous movie palace and we sit down amid the usual riffraff. A trailer is playing for an upcoming flick. It looks and feels like vintage Luis Buñuel.

But despite the grindhouse quality, it's futuristic footage featuring myself, alone in my Seattle hotel room, sweating and drinking and masturbating. The entire audience is laughing. Except for me.

MIND GRINDHOUSE

The movie trailer my sexy Spiritual Guide and I are watching in the seedy 42nd street theater circa 1982 continues with me leaving my hotel room and venturing out into the dark, deserted streets of 2020s Seattle amid a global pandemic that has probably infected everyone on Earth, even me. I watch myself enter The Last Call, tiki bar of the damned. Jesus. This is one of those goddamn "trailers" that shows every highlight of the actual movie. Except I've already lived this movie, or I will, yet again.

I need to counter-program the apocalypse. This detrimental projection is killing me. Unless of course I'm already dead, as I'm beginning to suspect.

But I'm a lousy detective who often reaches the wrong conclusions based on ambiguous circumstantial evidence, a professional flaw which ironically works in my personal favor given my present predicament. My own ineptitude gives me hope.

Except at this point in my timeline, I'm not yet a detective. I'm a pop culture journalist covering cinema and music for a local underground rag, often hanging out at CBGB, watching New Wave and punk bands. That's how I met Rose, or will meet her very soon. Again. But now I have her number, just like the Phone

Phantom has mine.

Phone Phantom. Rose. Detective. I know these words. But their meaning is starting to get fuzzy. Even the images on the screen feel like fiction, though they're allegedly from my own future. I recognize myself as an older man from the vantage point of reclaimed youth.

The ethereal beauty beside me is just smiling with her hand in my crotch.

The "preview" finally ends with my character drowning himself in the black ocean. The audience cheers. They're glad I'm dead and the lengthy preview of coming distractions is over.

Maybe I should be, too. But I'm not, even as she strokes me till I climax in tandem with my own onscreen demise.

There must be more to come than this.

That's when I realize I'm alone, jerking off in public like the rest of the raincoats.

META GONZO

Whoa. What was that?

I need to focus. I'm too young to be this disoriented. I can hear the Blasters playing. I'm inside Ships Coffee Shop in Westwood Village, L.A., drinking my coffee, brought to me by my favorite waitress, Dorothy. By the time she brings my fried egg sandwich I'm listening to the B-52s. I'm right where I belong.

But who am I?

Was that an epic vision of the story I'm writing? It's already disappearing from my consciousness. I recall a guy being caught in a pandemic some time in the distant future. A private eye who walks dogs? He was from New York, though. Lived in San Francisco for a while. Moved to Seattle. I was born in Manhattan, never been to those other two. Not yet.

I just watched *Blade Runner* here in Westwood, at the Bruin Theater. Third time already. I see a lot of movies repeatedly. *Dawn of the Dead* seven nights in a row. I have little else to do. I'm alone most of the time, writing and dreaming. Night and day.

This was different. It's like I was this guy. Or he was me. I've already forgotten his name.

Now I can't remember mine. I panic.

I think of a line from the movie I just saw: "*All those moments will be lost in time, like tears in rain.*"

Outside it's still sunny. I caught a matinee to save money since I'd seen it twice already.

I sit and finish my sandwich. Dorothy brings the check. I head outside. It's dark already.

How much time have I lost?

I head back to my apartment. It's near my other favorite haunt, Dolores' Restaurant on Santa Monica Blvd, across from the Nuart Theater. I'm going there tonight to see *Eraserhead*. Again.

Inside my little room I lay on my bed and close my eyes. Suddenly I feel like I'm inside the movie the guy in my dream was watching in a Times Square theater. My heart starts racing. I sit straight up, afraid to fall asleep, because I'm not sure where I'll wake up...

ANYWHERE BUT THERE

I fall asleep despite my contrary efforts. When I wake up, I make coffee, drink it, then wander outside into a foggy, desolate alternate reality. Still can't remember my own name. I can't even tell what era it is, much less the exact time. Westwood Village is completely deserted.

Well, not completely.

A young, beautiful girl whom I instinctively but not distinctly recognize approaches me with a smile and takes my hand. Following those basic instincts, I yield all control. She is wearing knee-high boots and a tight, one-piece dress with a Mod pattern. It's like she stepped out of another dream and into mine.

She leads me into the Bruin Theater. No one else is around. But something is playing on the screen. It's a movie of the movie inside my head, actually inside my character's head. I'm watching him watch himself on the Times Square theater screen, weeping and masturbating in both realms.

"What is this?" I ask her.

"It's the movie of your book, and your life."

"My life?"

"Eventually. They will merge."

"I'd rather merge with you."

She unbuttons my shirt, loosens my trousers, lifts up her dress, and straddles me.

"I want to give you something to remember me by," she whispers as she slides up and down, in between deep kisses. "Even though, you will forget for a long time. But this is where it all begins."

"Where what begins?"

"The End."

I close my eyes as I climax. Big mistake.

When I open them, I remember who I am. Vic Valentine. Back in the Seattle hotel room, sometime in the distant apocalypse. It's dark outside, though still daylight. I'm drenched in cold sweat, but my flesh is hot. I reach for the beside bourbon, take a swig. My pants are around my ankles, my hands and thighs all sticky.

Back to the old new normal.

But I'm not alone. There is a woman sitting in a chair across from the bed. I recognize her, though she is older.

"Hi Vic," she says.

I nod, not sure if she's real. "Rose."

BURY THE PAST WITH A HATCHET

She isn't the Rose I knew. I'm not sure I ever really knew her. Her sudden presence in my room doesn't throw me. Nothing throws me. I'm too heavy with regret.

"I'd ask how you got here, but I'd rather just know why," I say to her, sizing her up. She's aged gracefully. That's when I notice she's stark naked, like me. Did we just ball? You look beautiful, anyway."

"You look like shit."

"That doesn't answer my question."

"I've been thinking about you since the world collapsed. I thought of calling, but I wanted to say goodbye in person."

I wonder if she was the one leaving me musical messages. "Why? Are you dying?"

"Who isn't?"

"I mean, soon."

She looks away as her eyes mist over, sipping a drink she poured herself from my cabinet. All I keep stocked is booze. I guess I did go out and refill my supply, then returned and fell asleep, jacking off as usual. The rest was a dream. Or maybe this is just another part of it. I can't say I give a damn anymore. I'm just going along for the ride. For all I know, I'm looking at the driver.

"Really, how did you find me."

"Your wife told me."

"Oh yeah? How'd you find her?"

"We're old friends."

"You're kidding."

"I'm too tired to tell jokes."

"I'm too tired to laugh. Where is she?"

"Around."

"Is this a dream, Rose?"

"Maybe."

I go to the drawer, pull out my .38. "Only one way to find out."

I turn and shoot her in the forehead. She doesn't even blink. The wound still bleeds, though. Down her face, through her cleavage. I get a boner.

"Damn. I knew it."

"You like zombies and vampires and all that crap. I'm merely fulfilling a fantasy."

"So I've lost complete touch with reality."

"I don't think you two ever got along anyway."

"If you're not real, am I? Is anything?"

"It's all an illusion. Matters in the moment. Then it's gone."

And suddenly, so is she.

Sadly, I'm still here.

THE MIRAGE IN THE MIRROR

I just killed the former love of my life. But she was already dead to me anyway.

You could say I took a big chance. But in a world of zombies, shooting someone in the head could also be considered an act of mercy. For the shooter as well as the victim. Of course, Seattle homicide dicks might not agree with this philosophy. But they were nowhere to be found since the cops got defunded and the pandemic started wiping everyone out, including the killers who would've never been found anyway. Most cases of violent crime go unsolved. Like the one called Life. Mine, anyway. Justice is the ultimate illusion.

The fact that Rose vanished like smoke shortly after I blew her brains out solidified my theory. I wasn't even relieved. I knew she was a mirage. Just like the one I'm looking at as I stand in front of the mirror, watching myself disappear, but slowly.

I flash back on how we met, without actually taking the trip this time. I cough, sweat. I feel dizzy. I lie down. My life is passing before my eyes, but it's taking me with it, in and out of time and space, with no apparent pattern, for no reason. I have no idea whether I'm dreaming right now. That's why plugging Rose was such a risk. But then plugging Rose was always a risk.

For all I know, she started the pandemic with a STD. The gal got around, long before and after I was in the picture. But also while I was in the picture. That's one reason that picture got smashed.

I don't know the reason I never stopped loving her anyway.

There is a knock on the door. I say "Just a minute," then throw on a shirt and pants, the .38 cocked behind my back. I open the door and there she is, in the flesh.

My wife. Val.

I lower my gun, stunned by her radiant beauty.

She keeps her gun trained on me, though, aimed right at my heart. It's my most vulnerable spot.

MONSTERS IN THE CLOSET

"Is that thing loaded?" I ask Val as she walks in and shuts the door, gun cocked.

"Only one way to find out. Is your thing loaded?"

"You mean…" I belatedly notice I'm not holding a gun, just my cock, sticking out of my trousers. I gave up my .38 long ago. Rose was never here, I never shot her, because I never pulled that imaginary trigger.

The .45 Val redirects from my chest to my crotch looks real enough to take seriously. I put my own biological weapon away, zip up, and sit down on the bed.

"You need to figure this out before I can let you go," she says.

"I thought maybe Rose started the pandemic with a STD."

"Her? Why not you? You became a bigger slut than she ever was, at least until you ran into me. The second time."

"Eventually, but she was first."

"You're such a child, Vic. This is why I had to quarantine you. To protect you."

"From myself?"

"Yes, and to protect others."

"From themselves?"

"From you."

"Why?"

"Because you're the source of the pandemic."

Val, wearing a tight scarlet dress and shiny black pumps with no bra and probably no panties, sits next to me on the bed. She kisses me, but with the gun in my crotch.

"You don't need to threaten me."

"I don't trust you, Vic. You're having another of your breakdowns. Only this one might be useful."

"To who?"

"The world. If you can only remember where you contracted this illness."

"Mental?"

"Physical. I've given up on the other one."

"Is this why I'm time-tripping in my dreams?"

"If they're dreams."

"Must be. In one, I was in L.A., 1982. I wasn't myself, but someone else, writing this story."

"You need to finish this story, Vic. Especially now that we're all part of it."

"Never been into plots. More of a mood person."

"Relax and open up, Vic." Val kisses me again, goes down on me, gun still poised to fire. I shoot first.

Always been quick on the trigger.

BRAIN PULP

Sonny Burke's bongos-and-theremin score for the obscure 1962 monster flick *Hand of Death* is playing inside or maybe outside my head as Val and I make love. She knows how to soothe me, body and soul.

When I open my eyes, she's still there, and I'm still here. Seattle. The Apocalypse. Which is all my fault, apparently.

I look at my beautiful naked wife, filled with my fluids, leaking from both ends.

"Aren't you afraid of getting sick?"

"No. I'm immune."

"How do you know?"

"Trust me."

"Why did you vanish?"

"I didn't vanish. I was keeping a close eye on you, as always."

"Most people don't care about others. I don't understand why it's so hard to have empathy. I have empathy, and I hate people."

"Many say human beings are made in God's image."

"Then He or She is a mess. No wonder the world is so

fucked up."

"You must correct this virus, Vic. Only you can do it."

"Obviously I'm still dreaming."

"Not any more so than the rest of humanity. In the end, it's all a dream. But this is as real as it gets."

"Are you saying I'm Patient Zero? I thought this shit got started in a Chinese wet market, or from bats."

"Initially. But it mutated, long ago."

"Why is that my fault?"

"Maybe you fucked an infected vampire woman."

"Rose?"

"No. Me. Back in 1982. That's actually the first time we met, when I was very young. You were in L.A. with Rose. You ran into me while walking around Westwood, alone. I mesmerized and seduced you. It wasn't hard."

"Why?"

"Because you're mine. You always were."

"You put a curse on me?"

She stretches out on the bed, nude and sweaty. "You call this a curse?"

"You gave me a virus."

"Not on purpose."

"It took a while to spread."

"Yes."

"So you're a vampire woman."

She smiles slyly. "A bat bit me when I was a child. In Mexico."

"Sounds like a horror movie."

"Life is the real horror movie, Vic. And right now, you're the star."

HOT AND DIRTY

I look out the window. Everything is radiating nuclear orange due to the wildfires engulfing the region, perhaps the world. At least the hotel has air conditioning.

"It's hot and dirty out there," Val says, still nude and spread eagle on the bed.

"In here, too." I climb on top of her and we make love again, because why not.

I fall asleep. When I wake up, she is still present. I am beginning to suspect I'm not hallucinating this reunion. Which means it really is the end of the world. If Val is right, I will take either the credit or the blame. Still clueless what I can do to solve Armageddon. I'll be The Last Man on Earth, like Vincent Price, warding off vampire zombies by day. Except I have The Last Woman on Earth, like the unrelated Roger Corman movie. Things could be worse. At least for me.

"I don't understand how I could've started all this, much less stop it," I tell her as we snack on whatever is left in the mini fridge, downing it with the rest of my bourbon. "I didn't fuck everyone on Earth."

"I gave it to you, you gave it to someone else, long ago. Now here we are."

"Why didn't you tell me sooner? That would've prevented the spread."

"I didn't know until it was too late. First I wanted to get you isolated."

"How can you be sure it's me?"

"Feminine intuition."

"Not very scientific."

"It's Nature. That's why I trust it."

"But I feel better now."

"But you're not."

"How so?"

"Look in the mirror again."

I turn and see myself as the monster I truly am. My face and body are covered in lesions, my flesh is green. I look like the living dead. Behind me Val still looks perfect. She is truly ageless. Magical.

"How could you make love to me like this?"

"I can still see the real you."

"Why couldn't I see this sooner?"

"Denial of the truth. The most ancient epidemic."

"What now? Like I told that quack, I'm not a scientist."

"Think."

WALK IT OFF

I close my eyes and concentrate, as Val suggested, struggling to remember the crucial clue linking my miserable existence on Earth with its currently critical condition.

I got nothin'.

When I open my eyes, Val is no longer Val. She's that phantom amalgamation of all my feminine fantasies, corporeal and cinematic, that took me on the magical misery tour through my own past. Except now she's wearing a black silk robe open all the way so I can see her ivory flesh, bosoms and bush. She's smiling at me with fangs that drip blood down her curvaceous torso. She holds out her arms, beckoning me. I'm tempted to dive into this erotic abyss of fatal bliss. But I have a case to solve.

First, I gotta get the hell out of here.

I throw on my sharkskin jacket and skinny tie. When I turn to give the hotel room one last look, she has reverted to a naked Rose with the gory hole in her head, staring at me with moist eyes.

"Don't go."

"Don't follow me." It's hard to leave. I dread more loneliness.

I'm down the stairs and out on the streets, which are full of smoke and fires. Masked looters are vandalizing what's left of the boarded up businesses, and ravenous zombies are attacking and devouring the looters. I look like the undead so they leave me alone. The skies are red with the atmospheric reconnaissance of ravenous wilderness flames encroaching upon what's left of civilization.

Inside my head, I envision a totally different world, one of jazz and cocktails and romance, downtown bustling with healthy pedestrians, skies blue with fleecy cumulous clouds, a crisp autumn breeze soothing my soul. In my delirium I hear "Hush" by Deep Purple. I don't know why, but it makes me happy, even if it's an illusion.

It's all an illusion. I just have to find the one I can live with.

I don't have a car, so I am walking all the way home, to Wedgwood, where hopefully, my real wife awaits.

If only I had a dog for company.

HEART IN FLAMES

Somewhere around or within me Nina Simone is singing "Sinnerman" as I make it out of downtown and see billowing smoke on the horizon near my destination. My heart begins racing faster than I can. The non-infected people that I pass and dodge are wearing masks, due to the pandemic or fumes or both. The zombies are not wearing masks. Their faces are already dead.

At last I stagger down the street in Wedgwood where I once lived with my wife. The entire neighborhood is engulfed in flames from the wildfires that are now destroying the city of Seattle. No one else is around, not even looters or zombies. The residents have long since evacuated, or died.

I am too late to save anyone. Even myself.

Dizzy with dread, I come upon the remnants of the midcentury modern house I shared with Val for a period of time I can no longer discern. My memories are nothing but hot mush in the bowl of my simmering skull.

Devastated beyond endurance, I sit on the sidewalk amid the smoldering ruins of my former life, a cool breeze wafting in off merciful Puget Sound. I hear Giorgio Moroder's "The Myth," a track from his score for Cat People, one of my favorites, released in the pivotal year of 1982.

I don't know why I keep hearing all this music, except for the fact my entire life is only a movie, and this is the soundtrack that I subliminally compose for myself, to make all the suffering and sadness palatable. In fact, I mentally repeat that refrain to myself, mimicking the marketing campaign for 1972's grindhouse classic *Last House on the Left.*

It's only a movie, it's only a movie, it's only a movie…

That's when a lost dog approaches me out of nowhere and licks tears right off my face.

I embrace the medium-sized mutt. I sob into his fur. He keeps cleaning my cheeks with his rough tongue. I wallow in emotional porn.

Then her shadow appears out of the macabre mist like an angelic apparition.

HELL IN HI-FI

I can't even look at Her walking toward me, just a shapely shadow in the smoke. I know She's just going to mess with my head and heart again. Even if She appears as one of my many sexual cinematic fantasies, I'm just not going to give in this time. Even if she morphs once more into the Love of My Life, who is now probably a crispy cadaver buried in the burnt wreckage of our former home.

It begins to rain suddenly, like Seattle often did Before, putting out the fire with gasoline. It pours down like liquid mercy as I sit there rocking back and forth, softly singing the opening refrain from a song popular in my childhood, "Delta Dawn," over and over, head buried between my legs. I can feel Her proximity. I'm just not ready to face Her.

I feel Her hand softly touch my sob-shaken shoulder, and I cringe. "Leave me alone," I whisper to myself, because I know I am now truly alone.

She kneels beside me, pets my hair, and I am already weakening. Okay, so what She isn't actually Val or Melinda Clarke from *Return of the Living Dead Part 3* or Anna Falchi from *Cemetery Man* or Mathilda May from *Lifeforce*. If it's all a dream anyway, why not embrace a mirage, especially if it hugs you back?

The wind picks up along with the rain. Finally I look into Her beautiful face.

It's not a fantasy. It's Val. In the flesh. I know it's Her, because I can truly see and sense Her. Those are Her eyes. You can't fake a soul.

She touches my wet cheeks, wiping away tears in rain, then takes my hands in Hers, and stands me up. She holds me in Her arms and we begin to slowly dance to Nina Simone singing "Wild Is the Wind." From somewhere, everywhere, nowhere.

With a kiss, she removes her wet dress, then my soaked suit. We continue dancing naked in the storm as the song grows louder, drowning out everything else.

Even my screams.

INTENSE INTOXICATION

As Val and I keep dancing amid the smoldering ruins of our home, we start gradually drifting. Not sure if it's upward or sideways or whatever, but our feet aren't touching the ground. We continue to embrace as we float to "Wicked Game," but not the Chris Isaak original, which I would torture myself with in my post-Rose mourning period. It's the Parra for Cuva version with vocals by Anna Naklab. It's more "Val" than "Rose," more "now" than "then," so appropriate for the occasion. Cheers to the celestial DJ.

"The world was on fire and no one could save me but you..."

Then I close my eyes and it's black. I think of all the cats and dogs I've lost. I envision them running towards me in that misty lakeside park in Windermere. I open my eyes and I'm there, but Val isn't.

I'm heartened by all my old friends surrounding me, including the dog that had licked my face when I first sat on the sizzling sidewalk. He licks my tears again, some from joy, some from sadness, the usual toxic emotional cocktail mix.

I close my eyes again as "Wicked Games" continues to play.

When I open them, I'm in my old bed, in our old home. I realize it's only a dream, but since I can no longer distinguish between reality and fantasy, I roll with it, right out of bed and into the living room.

There is Val wearing an open silk nightgown, offering me a Martini, as Bobby Darin sings "Dream Lover," but from an old school hi-fi system, not the fucking air. The place looks just the same, only something feels different.

I am wearing a silk robe, too. I sit on our sofa and sip my drink, instantly relaxed. Val knows how to make 'em. The dream dog sits next to me. So does a mystery cat.

The TV set is different. It's in black and white, and it's showing the Kennedy vs. Nixon debate.

Then it hits me.

Same Bat-channel. Different Bat-time.

SANCTUARY CITY

I'm no longer living in Seattle in the 2020s. I'm in Los Angeles, circa 1960. I'm fine with that, because Val is with me, and since she had decorated our ranch-style house midcentury modern style, it still feels like home.

Only when we leave the house in our blue Corvair — which looks like the one I drove around San Francisco in the 1990s, only brand new — do I realize the change in geography as well as the timeline. My memories are still all in the future. Somewhere across the country, in Brooklyn, I am merely an infant. But that's far enough away. I don't want to know that guy. I'm happier being this one.

We go to Ben Frank's on Sunset for breakfast. Oddly, they offer a vegan menu. I just go with it. It also seems strange they're playing the Blasters on the jukebox, considering that's a rockabilly band from the early '80s. I just hope I get to stay here a while, like forever.

I hear something ringing. A phone. It's in the pocket of my old sharkskin jacket, which blends right into the environment. Suddenly I'm shockingly conformist, sartorially speaking.

It's my cellphone. Those haven't been invented yet. But technically, neither have I. I answer it.

"Vic Valentine?"

"Yes."

"This is Harold Floyd."

"Who?"

"Your client."

"Client?"

"Yes. You're still on the case, yes?"

"Um…sure."

"You got any updates for me?"

"Not yet."

"Call me tomorrow with something, or you're fired." He hangs up.

I return the phone to my pocket. Val is eating her vegan pancakes happily. I sip my coffee as I dig into my tofu scramble and the B-52s perform "Planet Claire."

"Who was that?" Val asks. She looks dazzling in her snazzy pastel outfit.

"Client."

"What did he want?"

"Update on the case."

"Is this a new case?"

"Yes and no."

"I don't get it."

"Neither do I."

I look around. Black and Latino people are mingling

happily with Caucasians, though all are dressed per the period.

Only one possible explanation. I just have to figure out what it is.

PHANTOM BEYOND

I don't know if I'm asleep, or dead, or somewhere in between. This is all a dream, that I know for certain. I'm just no longer sure what defines a "dream."

When I dreamed while asleep, before my personal and possibly global inferno, I was never alone. My head was populated with people I saw once and would never see again, and yet we interacted as if we shared a lifetime.

Who were these strangers I knew so well in my dreams, who knew me too, that I forgot when I woke up? Is that what happens when this dream called Life ends? Everyone we thought we knew dissipates into darkness? Or do we just go on together, caught in an eternal loop of quasi-consciousness?

I hope I don't dream when I die. I hope I don't die.

Snapping back to the hybrid present, which is now the past I only imagined, a past that seems blended with the future I actually lived, I look at Val across the diner table and wonder if I only conjured her from my deepest desires, my insatiable libido, my need for maternal nurturing, which I missed being raised by my emotionally unstable and eventually mentally deranged mother. Val just seems too good to be true, and in my experience, if something seems too good to be true, it probably is.

But though she comes and goes without warning or explanation, she always returns, looking exactly the same. She is ageless, while I am not. And she's always been there, long before we actually hooked up, even before we officially met in San Francisco, early 1990s.

I now recall our very first brief, carnal encounter here, in this city, Los Angeles, in 1982. The Future from this perspective. When I was very young. Right now I'm at the dawn of the Sixties, in both the chronological and historical sense. Yet I feel so vibrant. Because of Val.

Maybe she is a vampire. I don't care.

All I do know is I remain Vic Valentine, Private Eye, and I'm on the case of my Life.

THE WANDERING CLUE

When my mind wanders I usually follow it. It takes me to some unusual places. Though now in this new normal, nothing seems that odd. It may just be one epic dream within a dream within a dream, as a certain Poe boy once put it, but it just doesn't feel like it, because for one thing, I'm too conscious of my surroundings and just how surreal they are, which means shouldn't this self-awareness have made me snap out of it already?

If I'm not dreaming, why don't I ever sleep?

I experience brief periods of blackness, possibly unconsciousness, which may be sleep, or some semblance of it, like after I made love with Val last night, here in Los Angeles, 1960. Or that's what I surmised based on several clues, like the Nixon-Kennedy debate on TV last night, meaning the dark previous to this light.

But then I get a text message on my cellphone to meet someone at the Theme Building at LAX. While construction began in 1957, it didn't open till 1961.

"I have to go meet someone," I tell Val as she gets the check. Some things never change.

"Who and where?"

"Not sure who, no caller I.D. But they texted they have the clue I've been looking for."

"Which is?"

"I haven't a clue."

"Where are we going?"

"LAX. Theme Building."

"That isn't open yet."

"So I thought."

We leave Ben Frank's, climb into my brand new Corvair which is basically the same one I drove around, or will drive around, San Francisco in the 1990s, and head for LAX. Sinatra is singing on the radio.

In a few miles we drive through an autumnal neighborhood that reminds me a lot of Seattle. I can see the Space Needle in the distance.

"I think we're lost," I say to Val.

She puts her hand on my arm and says, "At least we're lost together."

We pass through Seattle quickly and arrive at the Theme Building at LAX. Esquivel music is playing in the elevator as we head up to my mysterious rendezvous.

VIEW TO A THRILL

The restaurant at the top of the Theme Building reminds me a lot of the SkyCity Restaurant at the top of the Space Needle, which I frequented often until the clueless owners closed it after the completely needless, ultimately tragic renovations began in futuristic 2017. They totally ruined my favorite edifice, morphing it from a Space Age icon to a family theme park. Same as Vegas, which went from being Sin City to Disneyland in the Desert. In this alternate mishmash of time and space, perhaps SkyCity and Sin City both live, though technically the Space Needle won't open until 1962. Next year. At least from my current, randomly shifting perspective.

Meantime, Val and I are both preserved in the prime of our lives, so I'm in no rush to solve this case, nor overly anxious for that promised clue.

The restaurant is rotating slowly, alternately giving us spectacular views of Los Angeles 1961 by day and Seattle 1962 by night. Impeccably dressed people of multiple ethnicities are co-dining in the restaurant, enjoying perfectly constructed cocktails, lounge music spanning four decades playing on the sound system, from Martin Denny to Combustible Edison. It is an amazingly enlightened era, if chronologically ambiguous.

I look up at the big TV screen behind the scintillating bar. Though the images are in black and white, I see President Joe Biden and VP Kamala Harris hosting a news conference, sound off. They are both wearing face masks. I blink and it changes the channel to the original *Ocean's 11* from 1960. Just came out in theaters and already on TV.

A woman who looks like a young Eve Meyer, Russ's ex, wearing a tight leopard print pantsuit with her bountiful cleavage poking out like two scoops of vanilla ice cream packed into a jigger, walks up to me and hands me an envelope.

"A clue?"

She winks and vanishes like mist.

Inside there are two movie tickets for a midnight screening at the Nuart Theater in West L.A. I check the clock on my cellphone. We have all the time in the world.

MENTAL MIDNIGHT

We finish our elegant vegan feast at the rotating restaurant. I am not eager to leave, but Val doesn't want to be late for the movie.

"You don't even know what it is," I point out. "It's not listed on the ticket. Only the time and place."

"It doesn't matter. You love all movies."

"I can no longer distinguish between dreams and movies, between reality and fantasy. And I no longer care. As long as I have you."

"Even if I'm not real either?"

My heart clinches like a fist. "Aren't you?"

"Does it matter? As long as can see and sense me."

I shed a tear of fear.

"Life is just a fever dream, Vic. Movies are merely manufactured dreams we enjoy within this dream."

"Yes."

"Do you miss the world as you knew it?"

"No."

"Why not?"

"I am deeply disenchanted with humankind. I prefer

animals. I don't like tribes. I like being alone. Except for you, and the animals."

"I understand."

"I'd rather be here. In this desperate city. With you."

We leave the Theme Building and return to the Corvair, then drive to the Nuart. I instinctively know the way. It's the theater where I will meet actress Linda Kerridge from the 1980 film F*ade to Black* in 1982.

Wait. That isn't me. That's someone else's future memory. I block it out.

At the theater, which is across from one of my favorite L.A. restaurants, Dolores', I notice the marquee advertises two popular midnight movies: John Waters' *Pink Flamingos* and David Lynch's *Eraserhead*. I remember seeing them both, back in New York, but that hasn't happened yet, nor have these movies even been made. There is a line of sartorially correct patrons outside the door. We join them.

The lobby looks the same as I remember it from my few visits. I am not sure which movie is playing since I don't know what day it is, much less year.

Once it starts, I see it is *Eraserhead*. However, Val tells me she is watching *Pink Flamingos,* simultaneously.

Even here, we co-exist in parallel dimensions.

WHAT I DO TO KEEP HER HERE

When you're losing a loved one, everything is distilled to its essence, and time itself never seems more transient and precious.

I remember taking care of one of my cats when she had kidney disease. Treatment was expensive, but her health was my only concern. I had to keep her with me as long as possible. But was it for my sake, or hers? Was I being selfish in prolonging her pain? I wasn't sure. She only returned my love with hers. Until she was gone.

This is how I see the woman next to me in the theater, which is very dark. It seems as if no one else is around now. They've disappeared or disintegrated into shadows. I squeeze Val's hand to make sure she is corporeal, that I am sentient. Both of these seem to be true, so I believe them. I just want them to stay true forever.

But this slipstream consciousness keeps me on edge. I have no control over my own circumstances. I know I am on a case. I just don't know what I'm supposed to solve. I assume it's the origins of a pandemic that will afflict mankind in the next century, the one I was living in before now. But "now" is a fluid state, never static, constantly dissolving into the past, while the future remains eternally elusive.

I don't see how anyone exists without going insane.

I feel a buzz in my pocket. I had turned off the ringer. As far as I know no one else around me can even conceive of a portable phone. Except for my client, Harold Floyd. He tells me he is waiting out front, and to come alone.

I kiss Val and tell her I have to meet him but I'll be right back. She looks at me and nods sadly. I cling to her as if for the final time, but I must do this to save her, and everyone. I have empathy though I am a misanthrope.

Ultimately, this is for my own survival. I cannot live without her.

ZOOM OUT FOR PERSPECTIVE

"Get in you car," Floyd says to me. "I'll drive."

"Where are we going?"

"You'll see."

"Can I bring Val?"

"She'll be waiting for us there."

"But she's still inside."

"She's everywhere, trust me."

"I haven't finished watching the movie."

"You will. In twenty years. Don't you remember how it ends?"

"It's David Lynch. It has no ending."

"Exactly. Just get in the fucking car. Don't talk."

Dr. Floyd looks younger than he did the last time I saw him, at The Drive-Inn in San Francisco circa the mid-1990s, when I hit him. I feel like hitting him again. But I'm too curious.

We drive, listening to June Christy, Sarah Vaughan, Julie London and Blondie on the radio. Suddenly the scenery is all dark desert. We arrive at a Holiday Inn by dawn. There are cool cars parked in the lot. In the distance I see the neon glow of the Las Vegas Strip. It looks just like it once did, in my dreams.

"Why here?"

"Let's go to my room, and I'll show you."

The messenger who looks like Eve Meyer is lying naked on the plush bed. I turn and Floyd is gone. The Lady Eve beckons me. We make violent love. I pretend she is Val, but it really doesn't matter. I just can't stand more loneliness.

I drift into space. I see the Earth floating in the Cosmos. When I return, I am alone.

Damn it. A set-up.

I head out to the Strip under the bright blue sky. I can see the moon, full but pale, fading in the sunlight. We're all alone down here, in any time, in any place.

Aesthetically anyway it's still the early 1960s. I pull into the Sahara, where Louis and Keely are performing per the marquee. I give the valet my key, go inside, buy a ticket for the matinee, and order a Manhattan.

The show begins. The famous duo sing "That Ol' Black Magic." I feel like I'm in Heaven, though it's probably Hell.

Except I turn and there is Val, holding my hand.

DRY BREEZE ON A WET DAY

Sitting in the classic Sahara showroom, I comment on how I've always wanted to see Louis Prima and Keely Smith live.

Val contradicts me in low tones. "But that's Steve and Eydie, not Louis and Keely."

"Lawrence and Gorme? No way."

"*Ssshh*. Just telling you what I see and hear with my own eyes and ears."

"Second time you're looking at the same thing and seeing something different."

"Happens all the time, actually."

"Maybe you're just part of my dream."

"Maybe you're just part of mine."

My mind explodes again and I order another Manhattan. Val asks for a Vesper. Classy dames are timeless.

"I figured you'd rather go see the Rat Pack at the Sands," she whispers. Her sweet boozy breath gives me a boner.

"I've seen them. Oakland Coliseum, 1988. Figure this is my one chance to see these two."

"Steve and Eydie? You told me you saw them in Reno, years from now."

I sigh. "Floyd told me you'd be here."

"He lied."

"So you're not here?"

"I am now, but despite him. I figured his plan and sped ahead. He wants to separate us now that we're reunited. He wants you focused on your task and he considers me a distraction. It's all a ruse."

"I get it. So that woman who looks like Eve Meyer wasn't really you?"

Eye-roll. "Nice try, Vic."

"It's all a dream anyway, right?"

"Dream on, lover."

"Fuck me."

"Later, perhaps."

"And fuck Floyd."

"I just did, to distract him. He's asleep back in his hotel now."

I spit out my drink. "What? You fucked that old man?" A waiter asks me to keep my voice down.

"You're older than he is, at least here."

True. Floyd looks like a college kid now. I feel much younger than I was in the 2020s, like I'm back in my 30s. Val seems ageless, but she always did.

After the show we drive down the Strip. It's raining but

Val claims it's hot and sunny.

No Rat Pack at The Sands. The marquee advertises a surprise act instead: DEVO.

LUCK ME

While I'm watching Devo perform "Gut Feeling" live at the Sands circa 1960something, Val is watching Tom Jones sing "She's a Lady," circa 1970something, apparently, even though that song hasn't even been recorded yet, at least judging by the aesthetics of our current ambience. But I'm lost in time, while time has lost all meaning. We're all devolving together.

Afterwards I'm not sure where to go, because location doesn't seem to matter anymore, either. I've lost my sense of direction, though I still have my senseless erection.

"Where to?" I ask her.

"Back to my place."

I'm feeling lucky in the right town. "You have a room?"

"Yes. Drive."

We head down the Strip and out of town, into the dark desert. We arrive back at the same Holiday Inn where Floyd dropped me off.

Her room is his room, or at least the one where he left me with that facsimile of Eve Meyer. This makes me very uneasy. But I trust my wife with my life, since she is my life.

Inside we walk in on Floyd passed out on the bed. Or I think he's passed out. Then I notice the bloody pillow. I turn and see Val has a gun on me. But it's no longer Val. It's my Mystery Woman, the one who morphs into Rose or Val or Eve Meyer or a vampire or whoever she needs to be to wrap my brain around her waist like a belly bracelet.

"God damn it, were you ever really Val?"

"No, but she was, and is."

"When? Where?"

"That's for you to figure out, detective."

"You killed Floyd?"

"After I fucked him, yes."

"With that gun?"

"Yes."

I look at it closer. It's my old .38, but newer. Then I hear the sirens.

"You're not seriously setting me up. I'll just tell them it was you."

She laughs as the cops burst in the door and grab me. I keep screaming and pointing at the laughing lady with the gun. But they claim it's just me and the stiff as they wrestle the .38 from my trembling hand.

CONJUGAL CONJURATION

Locked inside the pastel Vegas jail, flanked by sharp-suited gangsters, moping in their own cells, I close my eyes, trying to either sleep or wake up. Like I said, I never sleep anymore. Don't remember the last time I did. I merely black out sometimes. When I'm in that empty space, I have no consciousness, no dreams. It's like I don't exist. I only know I'm still sentient when I open my eyes, and remember being out, but nothing from within that inner abyss. It's the Absence of Everything, including me.

Must be a taste of Death, previews of coming detractions.

Bursts of gunfire snap my eyes and mind open. The cops are shooting at someone who is shooting back, killing them one by one. The gangsters are laughing and yelling. One of them grabs a guard by the collar, snags his gun from his belt, blows his brains out, then takes the keys to free himself and his buddy, leaving me alone as they shoot their way out.

Then I see Val, stepping over all the dead cops in her bloody boots. She is wearing a tight black jumpsuit like Tura Satana.

I assume it's my Phantom Lady, back to torment me. She's certainly not here to bail me out. She doesn't need to. The smoking machine gun resting on her shapely hip paid everyone off forever.

"Gonna just finish me off now?" I ask her.

"I didn't come for you, Vic. I came from you."

"Sometimes with me, too."

"Come with me now."

"How do I know you're not her?"

"You don't. She can be anybody, anywhere, any time."

"So that wasn't you who killed Floyd and set me up?"

"No. I was back home, feeding our pets. Sorry I'm late. It took me a while to track you down."

"Who told you?"

"Feminine intuition."

"I don't know whether to trust you. Not that I have a choice."

"Trust yourself. That mystery bitch. She's only a product of your fevered imagination. She doesn't control this dream. You do."

"And you?"

"I'm taking charge of the situation. Let's go."

FLIGHT FROM IMAGINATION

There's a neon exit sign beckoning us from the end of a long, dark hallway. Holding Val's hand so I don't lose her, we head toward the door, or where a door is allegedly designated. It's all black except for the glowing letters signaling our imminent freedom.

Just as we're about to finally escape this nightmare, Val is torn from my grip, as if by a violent vortex. For some reason there are lightning flashes inside the hallway, or perhaps a line of faulty ceiling lights blinking on and off, like electrical power being gradually restored.

Monsters and zombies from my Id, the ones I saw roaming the streets of apocalyptic Seattle, begin attacking Val, ripping off her clothes, ravaging and devouring her flesh, like the finale of *Cannibal Holocaust*. But they don't come for me. One burst of light illuminates my hands, which are green and misshapen. They don't attack me because I'm one of them. Perhaps I always was.

Val's final shots and screams suddenly stop as the moaning, drooling, hideous hordes obscure her from my view. I have lost her to the fiends from the future pandemic, who broke the barrier and followed us to this idyllic psychic oasis.

Sobbing, I tentatively open the door and I'm engulfed

in warm, blinding light. I have trouble catching my breath.

When I adjust my eyes, I am staring up at fluorescent lights from a hospital bed, hooked up to a ventilator. I see Val outside the visitor's window, crying.

Inside, at my bedside, is the attending physician, an old guy who looks familiar. That's because his name tag reads "Dr. Harold Floyd."

A nurse in a shockingly low cut nurse's uniform who is a dead ringer for *giallo* actress Edwige Fenech is standing by his side, holding a dripping syringe.

Val squeezes my hand as the nurse injects me with the mysterious cocktail. She winks at me with a sly, sexy smile just before I black out.

I'm back inside that dark hall for a long time, though I don't know it. I don't know anything.

Some detective.

MEET THE AUTHOR

After my latest fade to black, my vision focuses on a shapely woman in midcentury attire sitting by my bedside, tapping away at an old school typewriter. I recognize her from vintage photos. It is famous *Playboy* model, writer, actress and feminist icon Alice Denham. In her prime, in the flesh. So as 007 quipped when he first laid his blurry eyes on Pussy Galore, "I must be dreaming."

"You're not," she says.

She hears my thoughts, apparently. Makes sense, since she's probably one of them, magically manifested.

"I do, but you also said it out loud," she adds, still typing.

"So maybe I'm dead. And you're my guardian angel."

"You wish. I only transcribe events for the record."

"Why?"

She shrugs, picks up a cigarette from an ashtray on her little desk, takes a drag, then sips whiskey from the tumbler next to the typewriter. The room is otherwise totally bare and antiseptic.

"I'm a big fan," I tell her. "I read your books. The memoir about fucking all those New York writers in the fifties, and the one about the alien centerfold, which I assume is fiction. What are you working on now?"

"Your life."

"So it's all your fault."

"Like I said, I'm only filing reports."

"To who?"

"None of your business."

"I never know anything. Especially about death. Except I must definitely be dead. No other rational explanation."

"Either we aren't meant to know what happens when we die, or there's nothing to know. Either way, we don't know anything for certain till it happens. Then it's too late to warn anyone."

"Who wrote that?"

"I did, just now."

"But it's me who just thought it."

"I know. I'm your ghost writer."

"So you're a ghost?"

"Or you are."

"Don't you know?"

"Only what you tell me."

"As I keep telling everyone, I know shit."

"But you talk a lot anyway."

An epiphany abruptly arises. "The pandemic isn't the

mystery. Death is. I'm supposed to solve that? Only one way. I'm not ready."

She gets up, leans over, and kisses me.

You know what comes next.

FOR THE RECORD

Lying together in post-coital bliss, a state I'm enjoying whether I'm actually in corporeal form or not, my celestial biographer Alice Denham resumes interrogation for her ongoing project, of which I am the sole subject. In one corner of the otherwise barren room, a topless Eve Meyer is playing jazz records for background ambience. She seems dreamy and detached.

"Just tell me about yourself," Alice tells me after some steamy sex. "I'll take dictation."

"Not touching that."

"That's okay. I'll touch it for you."

"I believe I'm already touched. In the head."

"Several times a day."

"Not so much anymore."

"Are you having trouble keeping it up?"

"My spirit?"

"It's all connected."

"If you mean what I think you mean, yes. I'm getting old. Hell, I am old. I mean, I'm never old when I'm here, wherever this is. I feel young and energetic. But

I can only sustain my mind, body and soul with fantasies now. I've given up on reality. Or it's given up on me."

"Everyone deteriorates."

"Not you."

"Because I appear how you imagine me."

"So you're not real."

"Reality is relative."

"I've heard that before."

"You've said that before. I'm only quoting you."

"The world outside and my body change. The world within me doesn't."

She scribbles something in her notepad. "Go on."

"That's all I got."

Alice gets up and starts typing.

"What are you writing? I haven't said anything."

"I'm writing what's going to happen next."

"I thought you were only transcribing my thoughts and deeds?"

"Sometimes I'm psychic. You're very predictable."

"You know me too well."

"You're an open book, Vic."

"I get the idea one of you is Val, and one is Rose. I just can't decide which is which."

"Perhaps we're neither. We could simply be

manifestations of your aging libido."

"Most guys even my age don't fantasize about midcentury pinup models."

"You're living inside your own alternate universe, a composite of all your fantasies."

"Does this mean I'm dead?"

"Wouldn't that be nice? Then you'd be in heaven."

"Unless it's the waiting room for the other place."

She just keeps typing.

THE COSMOS AND ALL THAT JAZZ

Suddenly the antiseptic hospital room transforms into an elegant, opulent vintage nightclub, replete with live music, cocktails and happy patrons. I'm still in bed, lying on my stomach now. That can't be good. I see Alice and Eve slow dancing with strangers as the band plays and the female vocalist sings "Key Largo." Nobody seems to notice me.

The singer is a white chick, but she sounds like Sarah Vaughan. That can't be right. My thoughts drift with the lyrics anyway.

I'm in Key Largo, Florida, on the actual African Queen. With me is actor Christian Slater. I don't feel like myself, but at least I'm out of the hospital bed. I can still hear the music.

Slater is on a cellphone, talking to his agent in Los Angeles. "I'm on the real boat, the one used in the movie...*The African Queen*...that's the name of the movie...what?"

He hangs up in disgust, looks at me and says, "He's never even heard of it. Kids."

I shake my head. Other than a dog and an old sea captain steering the boat, there's nobody else on board. The captain looks like my sailor statue named Ivar. I see sharks swimming in the water. Christian hands me a Cuban cigar after lighting one up himself. I accept, puff, but don't inhale. We dock at a restaurant called Tiki.

Inside it's a classic tiki lounge, right on the water. I follow Christian in, but then he disappears suddenly, like he was never here.

The tiki bar looks like the Mai Kai up in Fort Lauderdale, but smaller. The real Sarah Vaughan is singing "Key Largo" now, so it makes sense I can still hear it, though it seems to be an endless version.

Then I see myself in the corner, lying on my stomach, in the hospital bed. I go to the bar, order a Mai Tai. Looks like the early 1960s. No wonder Slater is gone. He hasn't been born yet.

I look up and see a sky full of stars. This must be heaven.

Except I'm alone.

THE MOVIE INSIDE MY HEAD

Next to my body in the hospital bed, over in the corner of the Florida tiki lounge, I see Alice Denham wearing a tight flower-pattern dress, furiously typing away, oblivious to all. My thoughts are still being mainlined into her brain. Our connection is telepathic and spiritual. I liked it best when it was physical. I am likewise wearing aloha attire while sitting at the bar, watching her writing my life, while I am apparently dying on my stomach. The stars in the sky where the ceiling should be are long dead yet stubbornly luminescent. Like me, perhaps.

I wonder if I will begin to flicker then fade out once my body finally dissipates. Just in case, I order another drink. A Zombie. The topless bartender is Eve Meyer.

Out of nowhere her husband Russ, also wearing a tropical shirt, storms up and punches me off my stool. "That's for fucking my wife." I hear someone laughing. It's Harold Floyd, also in cabana wear, on the stool next to mine. I guess he isn't dead after all. No more than I am.

Russ just leaves. Floyd, old again, acts like we never met, so I ignore him back. I look around at the other patrons, all familiar due to fame. Marc Maron is in a heated discussion with Hunter S. Thompson. Mickey

Rourke is having a beer with Charles Bukowski. Tom Waits is at the piano, performing "Blue Valentines." David Lynch is having pie and coffee with Marlon Brando. The waitress looks just like B movie scream queen Allison Hayes, wearing a skimpy sarong with her bountiful breasts barely contained.

Sensing my lust, she comes over and kisses me. I shoot my wad right there, so I won't be able to move for a while. Nobody cares. It's like I'm back in the real world. Except as usual, this all feels as real as it gets.

"Because if it's all a sentient dream, inside or outside your head, what difference does it make?" the bartender asks me. I recognize his voice.

It's Doc, from The Drive-Inn.

FUTURA

The bartender is definitely Doc, but he doesn't recognize me, making me sad. He looks like he's in his prime, back in the 1990s, or rather, far in the future. Obviously time does not define this dimension. Or my dementia.

"My name ain't Doc," Doc says. "It's Curtis. I'm no doctor. I can barely keep this job. I told the owner I'm from Jamaica so he'd hire me."

"Why does that matter?"

"Means I'm one of the good ones, you know? Like Harry Belafonte."

"I'm confused."

"I can tell."

"Is that why you said what difference does it make, if it's all a dream, dead or alive?"

"I didn't say that. You did. To yourself. I mind my own business, man. Want another drink?"

"I guess." I miss my old friend, and he's right in front of me.

Doc nods and starts making me another Zombie. I notice my tiki mug looks like George Romero. I look over to where my body in the hospital bed should be, with Alice Denham typing my story by my side. But they're gone, replaced by Salvador Dali painting a portrait of his nude model, Bettie Page. I guess that means I've finally left the corporeal plane, and I'm stuck here now. Not so bad.

Elsewhere in the tiki lounge, Mickey Rourke is in a bloody brawl with Charles Bukowski. David Lynch is now having pie and coffee with Jim Jarmusch, since Marlon Brando got up to dance with Marilyn Monroe as Debbie Harry and the Jazz Passengers perform "Call Me." Marc Maron has wrapped up his interview with Hunter S. Thompson and is uploading it to his WTF podcast via a laptop.

I hear a car honking, even though the joint was on the water when I entered. I get up, go outside and see a rocket-ship on wheels driven by Frank Sinatra. Dean and Sammy are in the back.

"Get in, kid, we gotta get back," he says.

"To where, the future?"

"As long as it ain't the Big Casino. Let's go."

I look inside at Doc and wave goodbye. He doesn't see me.

QUICKSAND OF CONSCIOUSNESS

In any dimension, I'm surrounded by images from the past and the future, which have apparently melded into one pre-post-apocalyptic collage-mirage. Everything seems like a ghost of itself.

Mainly I just want to hold onto my loved ones, Doc and the women and the animals, anyway, as tightly as I can, as long as possible.

I want to appreciate every day I have left with them. But as we grow old together, if we're that lucky, each day ends faster than the one before, till it's all an accelerating blur. I can't hold on to anything, or anyone. Everything and everyone just dissolves into the quicksand of consciousness. Eventually I'll be sucked into that whirlpool of oblivion as well.

In the meantime, it's sip or suck it up. Either way, I'm going down that drain with them. We're all on Death Row from the moment we're born.

"Lighten up, kid, before I crash this crate into a heavenly body," Sinatra says to me as we cruise through the Cosmos, Dean and Sammy cutting it up in the back seat, oblivious to my morbid contemplation, which is apparently being broadcast in stereo.

"Sorry, Frank."

"Mister Sinatra."

"Sorry."

"Just kidding, for Chrissake. Don't be such a bum. Life is too short for all this pointless pondering of the Infinite. Here we are, in the god damn Eternity of Space and all that jazz, and we still don't know what the hell is goin' on!"

"So why did you pick me up? I was fine where I was."

"No, you weren't. You were hallucinating a wet dream straight out of your suicidal sub-consciousness. I should know. I'm a 24 karat manic depressive. Sliding up and down that pole like a stripper on steroids. You gotta keep swingin' while you still can, kid."

"How?"

"A sexy dame is unhooking her bra after bringing you a bottle of bourbon and you need an instruction manual? Trust your instincts. Dropping you off here."

I wake up in my Seattle home next to Val, sound asleep. Pinup calendar on the wall says 2021.

BEFORE AND BEYOND THE END

Sinatra is singing "I Have Dreamed." But it's not from inside my head, just the stereo. It's still 2021. That's both a surprise and a relief. But it's only momentary. I know whatever visions I experienced while unconscious are only previews of the fate that awaits us all. We're always tottering on the brink of the abyss, whether we know it or not.

I'm at the breakfast table, sipping coffee, as Val sits beside me. We're both old, but she doesn't look it. I do.

"You had another of your psychotic breaks," Val tells me. "Like the last time, only worse."

She's referring to the period when I was going back and forth between an imaginary place called Planet Thrillville, where my evil doppelgänger, "Will the Thrill," tormented me. During this time Val put me up in a small room over in the Fremont neighborhood of Seattle, since it's one of my comfort zones. I was still able to maintain my regular dog walking duties and function fairly normally, except when I'd pass out and mentally travel to this alternate dimension where talking tiki statues, B movie monsters, living pinups, ultra-lounge decor and other fetishistic fantasies of mine merged into a cerebral oasis. Though never officially diagnosed or treated outside of Val's

103

emotional and financial support therapy, I assumed it had something to do with my exposure to exotic, experimental hallucinogens during an adventure in Costa Rica years ago. Washed down with lots of booze, of course. My drinking has since been self-moderated. I thought I was doing fine. Then all this happened.

"Was there even a pandemic?" I ask Val.

"Yes. Vaccinations are now underway. We're nearing the end of it soon, hopefully."

"So what caused me to freak out again? Was I infected? Or you?"

"No. But someone close to you was. Someone you haven't seen in a long time, but with whom I've stayed in touch, since she became my friend, too."

"She? Who?"

"Rose."

"Rose! Well, how is she now?"

Val sighs, looks into my eyes through tears, and says, "She's dead."

SHADOWS FROM THE OTHER SIDE

Often in order to see something right in front of you, you need to look right through it.

As I sit there absorbing the shock of Val's revelation about my old flame Rose being snuffed out, just another statistical casualty of the global pandemic, at a relatively young age (ours), the kitchen of our midcentury modern Seattle home begins to change in kaleidoscope fashion, morphing into my old office above The Drive-Inn back in San Francisco, to that Florida tiki lounge where I encountered all those celebrities, alive and dead, and Doc as well, though he didn't recognize me, to The Last Call tiki bar where I first met Harold Floyd, and back to the downtown Seattle hotel room where ostensibly Val put me up—again—until my latest episode passed. This one wasn't induced by psychedelic chemicals or alcohol, though. It was the trauma of losing Rose for the final time.

Actually it wasn't Val, but Rose's son Sammy who called and let us know. That's the last thing I remember clearly, at least in this dimension. I continue to ignore the shifting ambience, even as it turns into deep space, with the kitchen table floating in the cosmic expanse of nothingness. I just sip coffee, even when Agent Cooper of *Twin Peaks* joins us, and Val turns into a vampire, drinking blood from her cup, spilling some down her breasts, since she is wearing nothing but her soft skin. I know none of it is real. No more real than anything, anyway.

I think of Rose but I can't cry, not yet. Instead I think of all the cats and dogs I've lost, and then I look at Val, who now looks like young Rose, though I know she is not. I realize that everyone and everything around me will one day vanish, like none of us were ever here. It's all temporal, all an illusion.

Sinatra keeps singing "I Have Dreamed." I stand up, slap myself in the face, and then it all snaps back into sharp focus. Life is normal again.

That's when I cry.

THE ILLUSION OF POSTERITY

For years after my friend Doc died, I was visited by his apparition. Naturally this can be chalked up to delusional desperation, since for most of my adult life Doc wasn't just my best friend, but my only one, outside of my pets and Monica Ivy, whom I haven't seen in years. I miss Monica but am comforted by the fact she's still alive and well with her wife down in Portland. We keep in touch. That's how I know she's still alive. We almost hooked up for real once, but for whatever reason, after Rose, I had trouble connecting with women on a deeply emotional level. Commitment was not in the cards, only crass carnality. Then Val revealed herself as my longtime stalker, laying permanent claim to my heart.

But there is no permanence. The realization of this hard truth, especially as I grow closer to the inevitable end, disappearing daily in the mirror, has become too much for me to peacefully accept.

This is what my beloved wife explains to me as we drive around Seattle in my Corvair, which she magically recovered, just to soothe my soul and provide me with a link to my youth, even though my present life is much more tranquil. Except when I'm suffering these mental midlife meltdowns, which are really spiritual crises in the autumn of my years, not even late summer anymore.

I need to make it to and through winter. I always liked winter. But autumn is my favorite season. I want it to last forever.

Val fills me in on the details of Rose's death. She was on a ventilator when she gave up the ghost. Sammy was her caretaker. He tested positive but remained asymptomatic. He feels guilty that despite precautions, he contracted the virus during a routine food run and brought it home. Rose seemed healthy but it turned out she had some underlying conditions. I don't ask what they were. Doesn't matter now.

Life is the ultimate underlying condition, with only one possible outcome.

I need a drink. I kiss Val instead. While I can.

GREETINGS FROM THE FUGUE STATE

"Dreams are memories re-imagined."

This is what my highly educated and very hot wife tells me as we drive through the idyllic neighborhoods of Seattle. Everything seems normal. Well, the new normal, post-pandemic. No glitches in my perception. All systems go.

How boring.

I already miss my strange journey through my own psyche, though truthfully, for all I know, this present place and time are still only dominant tiles of my overall sentient mosaic. However bizarre my detours through dementia were, they didn't feel any less tangible, and my accepted reality is equally transient. The lines defining and dividing the external and internal states of consciousness remain blurred, fluid.

Then again, I don't want to go backward. I'll settle for mental postcards. Val is here, in the flesh, our pets are safe and happy in our home, and we're about to go out for french fries and martinis at one of our favorite spots, the Ballard Smoke Shop, followed by Mai Tais at Betty's next door. They miraculously survived the enforced shutdowns of bars during the pandemic, and for this simple pleasure, I am eternally grateful. If only I could freeze my life or whatever this thing is and simply exist in a loop, driving to Ballard where we once lived, haunt-hopping, then to the Corvair just to drive right back, endlessly. I guess we'd like to have sex somewhere at some point, though we're growing old and less carnal. I know. In the backseat of the Corvair.

Fact remains, my body is slowly disintegrating even while occupied. My spirit feels ageless and immortal, but all flesh will eventually rot. The dream is dying as it develops, moment by fleeting moment. So it's all precious.

When there are so few days left, even if they're still measured in decades, you don't want any of them to end. Ever.

"I hope Rose is happy, wherever she is," I say to Val as we sit happily inside the cozy bar.

"Maybe our spirits merged," Val says cryptically, and for a second, I see Rose. I'm filled with dread.

NO REFUNDS FOR SOULS

I blink my eyes a few times and chalk up the visual glitch to my martini. They make them strong here at the Ballard Smoke Shop.

Val kisses me and everything feels right again. I must be getting PTSD flashbacks to my psychosis.

Rose is still dead. She will always be dead. But alive in my mind, itself drifting towards oblivion, floating on a sea of booze. Alcohol hits me harder than it once did, because I'm softer. Punch drunk. But the punch is still spiked.

I look at one of the two TV screens behind the bar, which stream sans sound as tunes blast from the killer jukebox, programmed by Val since we're two of the few patrons here at the moment. It's a mix of jazz standards and New Wave rock, our favorites. We're in Heaven. Or so I wish.

To top it off, I see the ex-president in handcuffs on one screen, Elvis in *Blue Hawaii* on the other.

"The people in his cult sold their souls for nothing," I say, nodding toward the news.

"No refunds," Val quips.

"I'm glad we're just Elvis cultists."

"Well, he's dead, so we can make him anything we want in our minds. He lives only in our imaginations now. At least we can still hear his voice."

"Yeah. He doesn't feel dead."

"Not to us. But we're still on this side of the screen."

"Mai Tai time."

We head next door to Betty's. We drink and talk and kiss. The wood paneling and retro-marine decor are so comforting.

Then we climb into the Corvair to head home, except Val takes us to another favorite spot: the Shanghai Room in Greenwood, adjacent to the North Star Diner. They're both quite Lynchian.

The dark Shanghai Room has several screens set up where a single movie plays. Right now it's *Blue Velvet*.

"Maybe Rose is with Elvis now," I say. "They were both so young."

Val just smiles, watching the big screen. I look up and see it's only a mirror.

We are merely reflections of a projected reality.

MEMORIES OF DEATH

Loaded questions, empty answers. That's all I got.

Val and are I safe at home. We watch *One Flew Over the Cuckoo's Nest*, make love, and finally, I fall sleep, though now I'm afraid I'll wake up dead.

Oddly, I do not dream. It's all blackness. No awareness of time or space. For an indeterminate period, I simply do not exist.

It's only in retrospect, as I sit in the kitchen drinking coffee the next morning, gazing out at pastoral paradise, that I realize this passage of lost consciousness.

"I didn't dream last night," I tell Val. "It's like I was dead."

"Maybe you were."

"There was just nothing."

"Sounds about right."

"Aren't you scared?"

"Of death? No. We've all died before. Just not all at once."

"What do you mean?"

"There's the theory of reincarnation, of course, and the

idea that, to quote Poe, 'all that we see or seem is but a dream within a dream.' As you know, I don't subscribe to any particular philosophy. The truth will reveal itself in its own time, and I can wait. I'd rather just live in the moment, here, with you."

"It all slips by so fast, sliding into the same black hole."

"Are you getting depressed again?"

"I never stopped."

"Aren't you happy here now with me? That we survived that catastrophe?"

"Which one?"

"Take your pick."

"I am, but it's inevitable there will be another one."

She takes my hand and squeezes it. "As long as we have each other."

"Yes. As long as we do."

"You're still sad about Rose."

"And Sammy. He must be lonely."

"He has his partner."

"Sammy is gay?"

"I didn't ask. I just know he lives with a loved one. He'll be fine."

"So Love is all there is."

"Yes."

"Till the End."

"Yes."

"What now?"

"There's always something, Vic," Val says. As if on cue, there's a knock on the door.

"I'll get it," I say, feeling uneasy for some reason. I go to the door and see my old friend Harold Floyd.

It might as well be the Easter Bunny.

OUT OF THE PAST INTO THE FIRE

If you want something to happen, you have to make it happen. This was once my guiding philosophy. But then shit just started happening around me, and I couldn't avoid it. These circumstances beyond my control became the main catalyst for my ongoing existence. I'm just along for the ride.

Harold Floyd walks in like he's been in our house before. Judging by Val's warm response, I gather he has.

"You got old, Vic," Harold says to me jovially as Val takes his coat and he makes himself at home on our sofa. Val goes to the bar to make him a drink.

I can't argue with his observation. "Yeah. I don't know how I got so old. It happened too quick, when I wasn't looking."

"You don't remember me, do you?" Harold says, searching my face for a hint of recognition.

"Only from my nightmares."

"You mean in your coma."

"Or whatever it was, yeah. I guess you remember me, though."

Val puts on a LP. It's "Dream On," a song from my

youth, though I dislike the band. Of course I didn't realize it was Aerosmith the first hundred times I listened to it in a loop, mostly via my inner speakers.

We're all silent for a while.

"Been nearly three decades," Harold says finally, sipping his martini as Val, dressed in a slinky silk robe, sits beside the stereo. I'm still standing, rigid with shock.

"You mean The Drive-Inn, San Francisco."

"Yup."

"You're here to hit me back?"

Harold laughs. "No. I'm here as a client, potentially, anyway. I want to hire you for a job."

"To cure the pandemic."

"You're Vic Vaccine now? I want you to find someone."

"I'm out of that racket. I can walk your dog maybe."

"No pets."

"So who?"

"You. I want you to find yourself, Vic."

My sense of serenity dissolves like piss on a sunny sidewalk. I can still smell it.

Now Val is playing "This Corrosion" by Sisters of Mercy. I like the song and the band. She likes to set the mood.

HIP TO THE HYPNOSIS

My mother, who died alone in an insane asylum, told me she never dreamed while asleep. Like me last night. Does that mean she now senses nothing, forever? Is this the fate that awaits all sentient beings after this brief kaleidoscope of sounds, images, thoughts and dreams? Just nothing at all? What's the point of that?

"Don't ask me, Vic," Harold Floyd says as Val mixes him another martini. She finally offers me one, but I pass. I don't like drinking in the daytime, even if it feels like night, given the deep cloud cover over Seattle.

"You can read my thoughts?"

"No need. You said them out loud."

"I did?"

"This is why I called Harold," Val explains to me. "He's my mentor in both psychological and spiritual studies, and was even when you first him at The Drive-Inn. In fact, I sent him myself. Of course this was before you and I formally met."

"When you were stalking me."

"Watching over you from afar."

"Like my guardian angel."

"If you like."

"Beats psycho succubus." She looks downcast, and I soften my stance. "I'm sorry. But this is too much. I mean, the encounter you're both describing happened in a dream, not a memory."

"A repressed memory that resurfaced while you were in a dream state," Val says.

"So it was a coma."

"Partly. You were alternately in a fugue state, like the last time, so several of your experiences were contemporary, but filtered through your warped prism of perception."

"That is correct," Harold confirms. "You and I did indeed meet at The Drive-Inn. Your friend Doc was there. But you did not actually hit me, as you seem to recall. That's merely repressed rage seeking release in your subconsciousness. I was a convenient target."

"Rage? At who?"

"Life."

"Why?"

"Because you keep trying to figure it out, and it keeps stumping you," Harold says. "Rose's death literally blew your mind."

I look at Val but see Rose. It's all a mirage. I figured this out too soon to keep enjoying it.

Sucks to be woke.

MAI TAIS IN THE JUNGLE ROOM
WITH LAURA PALMER

I'm sitting in the Jungle Room at Graceland, sipping Mai Tais on a Witco lounge chair opposite actress Sheryl Lee. Seated on a tiki stool at the little bar is John Lurie, who nods at me. Rose and I caught his punk-jazz band the Lounge Lizards frequently back in New York circa the early 80s. Sometimes Rose and I would buy him a drink after the show. He looks the same as I remember him. I thought he had retired to a Caribbean Island to recuperate from some illness. But there he is, wearing his *Stranger Than Paradise* porkpie hat and a gaudy aloha shirt, quietly sipping his own tropical cocktail. Over the sound system Elvis tunes play mixed with Angelo Badalamenti's score for *Twin Peaks*.

I ask Sheryl why we're here.

"The thirtieth annual Twin Peaks convention," she says, giving me a puzzled look.

"But I thought that had been cancelled due to the pandemic? I was so bummed because I had my tickets and flight booked. Just for me. My wife was going to stay home and watch our pets so I wouldn't worry about them."

"What pandemic?"

I look around. "What year is this?"

She smirks. "Very funny."

Suddenly we're no longer in the Jungle Room, but the Black Lodge. John is gone. The familiar red curtains and chevron lined floor give me the creeps.

"What happened?" I ask.

"Nothing," she says as if in a trance, still sipping her drink. "Who's she?"

I turn and see Rose sitting on the other side of me, young and beautiful. "Did you see John?" she asks me.

"Yes."

The Lounge Lizards are performing in the far corner. I point. "This is weird."

Rose laughs, then Laura Palmer joins her. I don't. Suddenly Rose slaps me hard in the face.

Reflexively I close my eyes and when I open them, I'm back in my Seattle living room. It was Val who slapped me.

"Vic, we lost you again," she says. "Focus."

"I thought I was."

Harold Floyd sighs. "Hopeless," he says.

NOSTALGIA FOR THE APOCALYPSE

I already miss the pandemic, because at least then I had a reason to keep fighting for survival. Without that looming threat to my mortality, I'm locked in this mental loop, without a purpose for being other than sentient existence for its own sake.

Then of course there's Val. But I'm not convinced she's real, or ever was. I know Rose was real, when she was alive. Now that she's gone, she's just another phantom haunting my psyche. I can't touch a memory. I can only feel it.

"Val, I'm lost," I tell her. "I'm sorry. I can't seem to stay in one place for long. My spirit keeps roaming."

"No," interjects Harold Floyd. "Not your spirit. It's your mind that is the vagabond, wandering the wasteland of your past."

"Shut up," I snap wearily.

"Vic, you've been down this road before," Val says. "And you always come back to me, here, now. On this plane of consciousness. This is your true home, your true self, even if it keeps changing, because that's the nature of life. We all evolve. The devolve. You're trying to escape the cycle by withdrawing into your subconscious world."

"She sounds like me, so she must be right," Harold Floyd chimes in, but he's already on his third drink, and my wife makes them strong.

"Shut up," I tell him again.

"Vic, how can we—I— help you to remain with me?"

I gaze at her, still youthful after all these years, then reach out and touch her cheek. A tear rolls over my index finger. I put it in my mouth and taste it. "My senses tell me you're real. But they lie to me wherever I go. Unless it's all true. One dimension is as tangible as the next. There is no difference anymore. The borders are not just invisible. They're gone."

I turn on the TV and there I am, back in the Seattle hotel room, dying alone in glorious black-and-white. It's a rerun.

I change the channel, and there's Rose, smiling at me.

Nobody dies forever.

DISTRACTIONS FROM DOOM

Since we're at a psychological impasse, Val proposes a threesome with Harold Floyd. I tell her he's too old, older than me, even. There's nothing in it for her. But then Floyd removes his clothing and reveals a much more muscular body than my own. Not to mention a much more masculine member. It doesn't seem biologically possible.

"You been banging my wife while I was away, Doc?"

"You never left," Val says, also disrobing.

"We did it right next to your bed while you were unconscious," Floyd says as they embrace then get raw and primitive all over the living room floor.

I watch in a trance without engaging. I'd rather just witness Floyd in the throes of fleshy ecstasy inside and all over my wife. It keeps my life juices flowing. Val is equally enthralled. I convince myself it's only a dream, because they're all dreams, one blending into the next.

But even dreams can have real world consequences.

After all three of us have soiled the rug I throw Floyd's clothes at him and order him out. I'm not mad at Val. Since I wasn't always available to her, mentally or physically, I encouraged her to seek pleasure with others, male or female. Then she'd pull a vanishing act and tell me lurid stories of her various sexual liaisons with all types of strangers, fueling my wildest erotic fantasies. I got the idea she was just making them up for my benefit. Now I know she wasn't. They were all true, as true as anything can be, anyway.

Floyd picks up his clothes and heads out the door naked. "I wish you both luck," he says, drunk on the bodily essence of my wife.

"Why do you like watching me with other men?" Val asks.

"Because Rose cheated on me so much. She taught me to like it."

"It's not cheating if I have your permission."

"It still hurts."

"So why?"

"The mix of pain and pleasure keeps me here, with you."

She kisses me and I drown in the pool of her corporeal mirage.

NAKED IN A POOL OF BLOOD

"If that was meant to be an intervention on behalf of my sanity, it didn't work," I say to Val as we lie nude on the living room floor, basking in post-coital bliss.

She doesn't respond. I assume she fell asleep. I look over and see her eyes are closed. She is so beautiful I don't mind if she's only a creatively composed composite companion made manifest by the force of my lonely imagination. I reach out and feel her breast, since it's so still. It's cold to the touch. I sit up in a sudden sweat, gut clenched.

Then I notice the blood. It's seeping from a wound in her soul. Her eyes suddenly open and stare straight into eternity.

I get up and pace, smacking myself in the face. I shout out for our pets, though I realize I don't remember their names. I just summon "dog" and "cat." But nothing with fur and four legs responds. Nothing responds at all. I am alone in our house, which no longer feels like a home.

Burying my head in my hands, I concentrate hard in an attempt to leave this dimension and return to the one where I belong, the real one, where Val is alive, and possibly Rose, too.

But it doesn't work. My heart is racing with my brain towards the nearest exit.

Quickly I put on my suit and head out into the brisk Seattle night. I get in the Corvair and drive desperately into the pink and purple twilight on the horizon, hoping I'll cross over into the next zone and find Life.

But I just keep driving, and everything is eerily quiet and still. Maybe there had been a power outage. The houses and buildings are all dark. No other cars are on the road. They're all peacefully parked.

I turn on the radio and find nothing but static and silence.

Is this it? Am I truly alone in a Universe populated by shadow puppets to keep me company? Was I always?

I hit the gas and disappear into the darkness.

ETERNITY'S LOUNGE

The Corvair passes through the glowing Seattle sunset into the next dimension. I've literally broken the space and time barrier and yes, "literally" actually applies in this context.

My borders between reality, fantasy, dreams and memories are no longer simply fluid. They're non-existent. All of my sensory experiences have merged into one continuous journey towards an unknown destination, and ultimately the journey and the destination merge as well.

I pull up in front of a brothel somewhere on the outskirts of Seattle, or maybe it's San Francisco or Los Angeles or Las Vegas or no place in particular. Doesn't matter. The surroundings are dark and desolate. All I can see is the ranch style house lit up with blinking Christmas lights and a neon sign in the shape of a voluptuous feminine nude with a flashing neon arrow bearing the words "Enter Here" pointed between her legs.

The door is open. I walk into a gaudy red lobby area. Exotica music plays. The madam looks like Shari Eubank, star of Russ Meyer's *Supervixens*. Rose is there, though she's being portrayed by Alexandra Daddario, her doppelgänger.

I plop down in a plush chair as the ladies prance around and display the dirty goods. Each are dressed in long silk see-through gowns with nothing underneath except trouble. They also wear high-heeled slippers and lots of makeup. The aroma of their perfumed flesh is intoxicating.

Though delirious with desire, I feel like going John Wick on the joint.

I'm led into a back room which is just as ostentatiously lurid as the lobby. My clothes are removed and my private harem is suddenly in session.

Of course, like most things that seem too good to be true, it's a lie.

The massive bed turns into quicksand and I'm sucked into a vortex that whirls seemingly for centuries until I land back in my Seattle living room.

I look up and see Val, unamused.

She is holding a cocktail which she pours onto my face. Then she hands me Rose's death certificate. To remind me.

Life is a series of cross dissolves.

REFLECTIONS IN A BROKEN LENS

In the 2001 movie *Memento*, written and directed by Christoper Nolan based on a story by his brother Jonathan, the protagonist (Guy Pearce) has short term memory loss. It was supposedly brought on by the trauma he experienced after his wife was assaulted. He's on a quest to find her rapist/killer, but since he can't remember anything after a few minutes, he keeps repeating himself, guided by his own handwritten notes and bodily tattoos for clues.

This is how I feel now: stuck in a perpetual loop of *deja vu*, unsure where I am, where I've been, or most distressingly where I'm going, all the while bogged down by the sinking sense it doesn't matter, because I'll always wind up right where I am. Lost.

Seeing my dreams and memories as scenes from a movie that happens to star me is the only way I can make any sense of it, or at least endure it willingly. I've never been the suicidal type. Death terrifies me. I'm afraid I'll be all alone. At least now I still have Val and the memory of Rose. I hope I still have Val. If I ever did. Even if she's only part of the mirage, that's enough to sustain me until the abyss swallows me whole.

I see the opening titles for the Movie of My Life lately as being designed by Saul Bass in the mode of *The*

Man with the Golden Arm. But rather than Elmer Bernstein's thrilling jazz score for that movie, which was more me when I was young and thought I'd live forever, now for some reason I hear the theme to the 2017 movie *Lowlife* by some band called Kreng as the opening music, since it radiates urgency. Seems incongruous and disparate, but so is being both sentient and finite.

It's the acute awareness of one's own mortality that can drive you mad. You get old, you get scared. You make shit up.

Val sits beside me and strokes my feverish forehead, licking the alcohol and tears from my face.

She is my Life.

SICK VALENTINE

I am sick of the world. Not Life. So I decide to just go ahead and fucking live. Life is short but hell, so am I. That never stopped me from living before.

Val walks me to the Corvair. Everything looks normal. Not new normal. Old, boring normal.

Apparently I'd just received the second dose of the vaccine, sometime and somewhere between my ongoing fugue state and my more socially acceptable semi-conscious one. Most of the world has been vaccinated by now. I was too lost inside my own delirious grief to care or notice, a possible side effect of the drug, according to Harold Lloyd, per Val. I guess it's good news. Time to move on to the next inevitable stage: Slow death by natural causes. Not as dramatic a journey, but same destination.

Val takes us to a retro-rustic restaurant called Shelter in Ballard, which has a vegan menu, including quality booze concoctions. The waiter hands us the craft cocktail menu. I'm in no mood for fancy.

"No high falutin' bullshit. Bourbon on the rocks. Leave the bottle."

"The bottle is forty dollars."

"Never mind, beer chaser."

Two kinds of shots to get me through the rest of this corporeal train wreck. The third kind can be fatal if fired correctly. I'll try not to get caught in anyone's crossfire.

"So there's still a tiny chance we could get the virus, right?" I ask Val.

"There's a tiny chance of anything happening, Vic, good or bad. Mostly bad."

Somewhere in my gut I know I'm not going to go suddenly, but slowly, a long fade out after a series of inexplicable dream sequences, randomly edited together into a plotless, pointless mosaic of mood pieces. That's how I see my Life, anyway. And I'm the only one watching it, besides Val, my beautiful, beloved co-star and possibly director/producer/screenwriter.

"Just tell me one thing," I ask my brilliant wife, who has a PhD in Me. "Are you for real?"

"You mean literally? In the moment, yes."

"Good. All we got."

Life is just something you learn to live with.

WOKE

This whole time I thought I was the hero of the pandemic, humanity's savior. That's what I kept telling myself, since my reel life and my dream sequences exist not in a vacuum, but an echo chamber.

It wasn't mankind I was meant to cure, but myself. I'd been vaccinated against the virus, but I'm not immune to the insanity I inherited from my mother. Or so I heard.

Val, my sexy live-in nurse, tucks me into bed and puts on a movie for us to watch. *Memento*.

"Funny you chose this, I was just talking to someone about it."

"Who?"

"Myself, I guess."

"Well, you never know who's listening."

I think about that. I often get the feeling someone is watching me, so I tell the stories of my life to Him or Her. Probably just paranoid. Being both willfully and unwittingly delusional is part of my organic self-therapy. My dreamworld is the alternate state of consciousness I invented for myself, with the help of corrupted biological chemicals, experimental narcotics, and booze.

Something about the confluence of a global pandemic resulting in Rose's untimely demise with my advanced aging and accelerated awareness of morality sent my psyche into a tailspin. Like always, it took me a while to recover. This episode was the worst, since I thought I might not survive it, mentally or physically. My Guardian Angel was there to catch my fall, though.

After the movie I lie awake next to my sleeping wife, thinking about the movie I'd just witnessed. Not the one on the little screen. The one I'd just lived, and thankfully am still living. It's not the story arc I'd hoped for, but at least it's still playing. And I'm not alone. Loneliness is the epidemic with only one cure, and it's not something that comes in a syringe.

Finally I drift off to that alternate realm inside my head, but now it's calmer, less chaotic. No vampire sirens or zombies or haunted tiki bars. Just a mishmash of memories and mirrors, not mayhem and madness.

I'll miss these desperate fever dreams.

Made in the USA
Columbia, SC
23 June 2024